A CROSSOVER ADVENTURE

AN EVIL, ANTI-STEPBROTHER, HATE TO LOVE YOU NOVELLA

TIJAN

Copyright © 2023 by Tijan

All rights reserved.

No part of this book may be reproduced in any form or by any electronic or mechanical means, including information storage and retrieval systems, without written permission from the author, except for the use of brief quotations in a book review.

Edited and proofread by: Kara Hildebrand, Rochelle Paige, Amy English, Crystal R Solis

Cover designer: Regina Wamba, reginawamba.com

1

"Babe."

Nope. I wasn't hearing him. It's like he hadn't spoken, and I kept going, tugging Caden forward, my hand in his.

"Babe." A little more insistent. A little more serious. He was starting to slow down behind me.

Nope. Again. Totally ignoring. I kept trucking along.

"Summer." Okay. A little snip there, which I got because I was ignoring him and we both knew it. He pulled on my hand, halting me, and as I turned, his head was angled down, an eyebrow in the air, and he was giving me the look. *The look.* The one that was asking, 'What the hell are you doing? Are we doing?'

I got that look a lot.

"I just want to check out this bar. I heard that lady at the gas station. She said there's a mermaid here."

Caden barely restrained his groan, but he kept moving forward. Success. We were still going, and I'd already won in that brief movement. He and I both knew, but he was going to argue the whole way there because of... I didn't know why.

Male ego? Because he felt he needed to put up some form of protest? I wasn't sure, but Caden would go with me to see the mermaid in the bar, even though we both knew there really wouldn't be a mermaid, but who would turn down a chance to see a mermaid? Um. Hello. No one. Or no one should.

Let's all live in our imaginations, or as much as possible, because this world was hella dark at times. Let me get excited about meeting a mermaid even though I knew we wouldn't. Are you feeling me? I was feeling me. That's all that was important. Me feeling myself. And with that, I had a little bit more of a bounce in my step as we walked down the street to the infamous mermaid bar.

Also, I really liked having the chance to say mermaid. It's not something that came up in everyday conversation, so now it did, I was going to milk it.

Mermaid.

Okay. I was done.

I think...

Mermaid. One last time.

Done. So done.

I was getting annoying by now, but we were here. The M-word Bar. It was an older bar, a large blue wood sign hanging out from the wall over the door with a mermaid in white paint. I was so excited. I was vibrating, and Caden stepped next to me, his hand going to my hip and sliding around as he went past me, reaching for the door. He held it open, and I walked in first, feeling Caden right behind me.

It. Was. Everything.

The little girl in me who always wanted to be a mermaid was in heaven. They had paintings of mermaids everywhere. On the walls. The ceilings. The bar. Under the bar, it looked like an underwater sea scene with bubbles running up the length of it. I had no idea how they did that, but it was amazing.

And right over the bar was a giant mermaid hanging from

the ceiling. She looked suspended in time and air, frozen, but so beautiful. She took my breath away. And looking through the bar, there was a back section with a giant aquarium that ran the entire length of the wall. It went all the way up to the ceiling, and I would not be surprised if they had people put on mermaid tails and drop down for a show.

I was vibrating again, or I hadn't stopped.

The bartender gave us a nod. "What would you like?"

I breathed out, "Everything."

Caden smothered a laugh, stepping forward and giving our order. A beer for him. Something fruity for me, fruity and delicious.

The bartender gave a nod and started working. He was large and looked in charge, a white T-shirt plastered over his giant-sized chest and forearms. Dirty blonde hair was piled high on his head, in a messy bun, that made him look even more buff. Chiseled features. Ice blue eyes. A very prominent jawline with a little dent in his chin. This guy looked like he'd been born specifically to work in a mermaid bar. His gaze ran over both of us. "You're not from around here."

Caden nodded. "We're on a road trip, stopped for gas. Then this one heard a mermaid frequented this bar, and we had to come and see for ourselves." He gave me a little head nod, a fond tone coming from him.

The bartender studied me a little longer before a slight grin tugged at the corner of his mouth. "You should stick around. We got a little show coming up tonight." He slid Caden's beer to him, his hands reaching to start working on my drink. "Where are you going for your road trip? Got a tight timeline?"

Caden picked up his beer, coming to stand right next to me, his other hand resting on the small of my back. He wasn't answering, and I tipped my head back, seeing he was studying me instead as he took a pull from his beer.

"What?"

He finished, swallowing, those dark eyes already knowing because he knew me. "You're going to want to stay, aren't you?"

I flushed and my vibrating was back, because hell yeah. I gave him a dazzling smile. "Well, you do love me…"

His eyes darkened, dipping to my lips, and his hand flattened against my back. He sighed. "Looks like I need to look for a local hotel."

The bartender laughed, sliding my drink to me. "My buddy runs a place on the ocean not far from here. It's usually full, but he tends to keep an area open at all times in case he uses it. He's not around right now. I could see if he wouldn't mind making an exception?"

Caden tensed next to me. "It's a hotel?"

He nodded, pulling out his phone. "A small boutique sort of place, but people go mad over it. Can't guarantee he'll give you a deal, but it's a nice place. Everywhere else is going to be booked up since it's agate season."

I had no idea what agate season was, but I was down for a boutique hotel. I looked back up at Caden, saw he was giving the bartender an assessing look, which I got. This was a small town on the Oregon coast. We didn't know him. Didn't know anyone here, but the whole point of the road trip was for us to be adventurous. If worse came to worst, we could sleep in our truck since it was renovated to be a camper. It was awesome. Caden's brother, Marcus, was a big traveler so it'd been a gift from him and their other brother to Caden. The message had been to breathe a little and live since the business Caden started with his brothers was doing phenomenal. Though, it hadn't started that way. The first five years had been hard, and Caden took on the brunt.

Since getting the camper truck, this road trip was partly a gift from Caden to me as well since we'd had a miscarriage a few months ago. I knew it was his way of trying to keep me busy, keep my mind off the little girl we were going to name Circe. So a mermaid bar? Totally need to stop a night to experience this place. If it was making me smile, Caden would do anything to keep that going.

"Here's his info." The bartender scribbled on a piece of paper and slid it over. He held his phone up. "I'll send him a text, but you can check it out. It's legit." His eyes were sparking in amusement, but Caden took the paper and pulled up the website he'd written.

I gasped as he showed me. The place was amazing. Chic and sophisticated on the inside. A very cute building on the outside, a little dated, but the inside made up for it and there were pictures from the basement, a walkout going right to the beach.

Caden took his phone back and I knew he was going to do a search on the place, on the owner, etc. Just making sure everything was safe.

A beat later, the bartender's phone buzzed. "My buddy said that's fine. He trusts me. You can contact him at this number to figure out payment." He gave us the number, and Caden took it from there. He already knew I wanted to stay. The trip's purpose was to be adventurous and to lean in towards being spontaneous. This was exactly that. As Caden took his phone outside, the bartender went over to fill orders for other customers. I slid onto the barstool, sipping my drink. He came back a little later, pouring a drink, but asked me, "What are your names? Hope it's cool to ask?"

"I'm Summer." I nodded outside. "Caden."

He glanced at my hand. "Married?"

That's right. My fingers had swollen so I took my ring off, and since then, Caden asked for it. He was going to get it resized. "Yeah." I didn't explain anything about why I wasn't wearing my ring, and he gave an easygoing nod.

"Cool. If you're a fan of pizza, the chef here makes the best kind. Locals will start trickling in in about thirty minutes or so. It gets busy, and with the show tonight, the place will stay full." He indicated a corner table in the back section. "That has the best view. It's open now, so I'd grab it if I were you guys."

"Okay. Thank you. We'll do that."

He gave another nod before heading back down the bar again, handing off the drink to another customer waiting.

When he came back, I put in an order for the pizza Caden liked, and ordered a second refill for myself before heading for the table he'd suggested. My back to the wall, I turned so my feet were resting on the seat next to me, and I got comfortable. Bring on the pizza, another drink, and whatever this show was going to be. I was down for it all.

Caden came in a few minutes later, spotted me, and headed my way. A slight grin was back on his face as he took the seat across from me. "We're getting comfortable?"

"It was the bartender's suggestion, and I agree with him. This table has the best view." I informed him what else the guy had said and Caden was nodding by the time I was done. I asked, "All set for the place?"

"Yeah. The guy didn't want to talk, but seemed fine with it. We figured it out. It's not far from here." The bartender was coming over with my drink, and Caden watched as he did. "I asked Marcus to run this place too, see if anything weird popped up."

"Did it?"

His eyes narrowed as he shrugged. "Nothing that'll affect us. Think he was just being helpful, not setting us up for anything."

That made me feel better, and also the excitement just got even more. I felt like I was a full balloon and floating to the ceiling. Drinking with Caden was my favorite thing, or one of them. Mix in pizza, mermaids, and watching the locals? I was *in*!

Also, it was close to Christmas so the place was decked out in decorations. A giant palm tree was in the corner with little flamingos hanging from it.

2

The pizza came over. A second beer for Caden. A third fruity drink for me.

I was buzzing when the locals started showing up, and there was a whole other buzz coming from *them*. They were excited as well, and I was feeding off that. We were getting a few looks, mostly the women were checking Caden out, and I could not fault them. A few middle-aged ladies were giving him looks, but also giving me smiles because whatever I was doing, they were enjoying.

Not that I thought I was doing anything. Maybe they could just see my excitement levels because I was not hiding that.

After eating, Caden and I played darts. It was heated and competitive. The heat level kept getting stoked because Caden would stand behind me as I threw and I wasn't about to push him away. We'd been together all through college, been living together since, and we married five years ago. We also had two little girls, twins. Caden was doing his business, a tech company, but it was growing massively and I'd been busy going to graduate school. I was now doing post-graduate work, which

I got paid for, but it wasn't much. The last couple years had been hard so this trip had been a welcomed adventure.

We were reassured that the girls were good with my dad. *Repeatedly* reassured. The last I heard they were going gnome hunting in the backyard.

"Babe."

I'd been picking out music, but looked back. Another couple was at our table, standing next to Caden. It took a second for it to click who they were, but once I did, I was across the room in a heartbeat. Shay and Kennedy Coleman.

Caden and Shay had been friends first. Each knew of the other through university events, or knew of each other because while we didn't go to the same colleges, both were in the same social circle. Also, everyone at our school knew Caden and it was similar with Shay. He'd been the starting quarterback of his football team, and one time at a conference, the two hit it off over a beer. They'd been tight ever since.

Kennedy and I became friendly later. I heard about Shay, but it was a couple years before I met him, until one time, he and his wife were driving through and they stayed at our place for the night. I liked Kennedy, but I was also a little scared of her. You didn't mess with Kennedy Coleman. Though, she was hella loyal. But fierce. I was sure that came in handy with her career since she was a broker. Shay, I wasn't quite sure what he did. It was some sort of liaison person between colleges and professional football teams. He did a lot of traveling. Kennedy mentioned that a lot, if Shay was home or not.

Seeing them now, as I wrapped my arms around Kennedy for a hug, I had to wonder if Caden did this as a second surprise. "What are you guys doing here?"

Kennedy held me a little longer before stepping back, blinking rapidly. She tucked a piece of my hair back for me, a soft wistfulness flashing over her face before totally stepping back. "We're–"

Her husband moved in, bending down to give me a hug too. A strong hug. And firm. He murmured while he was there, "We're so sorry about the baby."

That had me choking up because that was so sweet of him. I stepped back, brushing a hand over my face, and moved right into Caden, who wrapped a hand around me, going to my hip. He tucked me close to him.

"Thanks for that."

Caden and Shay shared a look. I took a breath, beaming at Kennedy. "For real. What are you guys doing here?" I looked up at Caden. "Did you do this? Was this planned?"

He opened his mouth, but Kennedy said, "No, but kinda. He mentioned a while ago that you guys were doing this road trip and we're also up here in Oregon visiting my brother." She moved into his side, almost mirroring us. "Shay remembered, wondered if we were in the same area."

"I couldn't reach Caden, but I got a hold of Marcus. You must've just talked to him?"

Caden nodded. "Yeah. I called him about a place here, if it was safe or not."

Shay nodded too. "He mentioned that place, and it's good. It's better, actually. They're usually booked out years in advance so you kinda hit the jackpot."

"How do you know this?" I asked.

Kennedy replied, "My brother lives in the next town up, but we come here a lot. The place you're staying at, no one knows the owner. It's run through a vacation company."

"No one knows the owner?" I glanced beyond Kennedy, to the bartender. A piece of his hair had slipped out so he had a strand covering his forehead and eyes. As he worked, he kept reaching up to brush it aside and it'd only fall back in place. It didn't seem to deter him. He kept working, which he needed to because the place was nearing standing room only. His hair was a bit messier too, with stray strands flying around.

"We don't think he's around that often, but it's fine. Everyone who stays there raves about the place."

Well, that made me feel even happier. I asked, "You guys are staying, right? There's a show happening here sometime."

Kennedy laughed, nodding. "Gage might come later tonight, but yes. That's the plan."

Gage was Kennedy's brother, who'd I forgotten lived up here in Oregon. He took a job with a local company. I couldn't remember what he did, but as we settled back around the table, I asked Kennedy how the rest of her family was doing. Shay's as well. I was on my fourth drink when Kennedy was telling a very in-depth story about how potty training their little boy was going. He liked to yell for his butt to get wiped and would bend over to be helpful. Shay demonstrated the pose, and I almost fell off my stool from laughing so hard.

The table beside us overheard, and joined in, telling stories about their own children. It wasn't long before the four of us were mad friends with their whole table, who were locals and who all wanted to know about us as well. By that time, Gage showed up, and a whole camaraderie fell over our tables because he bridged the gap between tourists and locals and all was well in the Mermaid Bar that night.

Or for the moment.

3

I was six pink drinks in and bouncing my butt to WAP when suddenly the music cut off. A protest rose up from the crowd, but immediately the lights went dark. A spotlight tracked to a small stage set next to our table. An excited hush came over everyone.

My heart was palpitating. This was the mermaid time? My palms were sweating.

Dry ice filled the room, the fog covering our feet first and rising up. Then, a small techno beat started. Slow and small. It grew. And grew. And grew. And I was starting to jump up and down, my hands clenched together against my chest. Everyone else was beginning to move too, until suddenly clash, bam, a cymbal smashed and the music built to a super-fast crescendo.

An explosion.

Glitter and confetti threw up everywhere in the room.

The music was now going full blast into a whole techno dance song. People were going crazy, and so was I. My hands were in the air. I was twirling, trying to catch some of the confetti in my mouth. Kennedy was laughing next to me, trying to cover my mouth.

We'd been dancing for the last two hours, along with some other ladies. Gage joined periodically, but he was off with some girl. I looked, craning my neck, and yep, he had a girl pressed back against the bathroom hallway wall.

Caden and Shay were behind us, still at the table, but standing at the end and half leaning.

The bar wasn't that big.

The dance floor was right next to our table, so we weren't far from them. The other ladies had both leaned over at one point during the dancing, asking who we were, who the hotties were behind us.

I didn't blame them.

Caden had these seriously dark and beautiful eyes. A snake tattoo on his arm that looked like a real one, enough where it startled a few people. Chiseled cheekbones that hadn't softened with age. His very no-nonsense demeanor that gave him an air of authority. I'd be checking him out too if I wasn't married to him.

And Shay was right next to him.

Tall. Broad shoulders. Dark blonde hair and blue eyes that looked trimmed with ice. The guy could walk any runway, plus he'd been a DI quarterback. The athleticism still emanated from him. Two of the ladies were in their fifties, and the other three were in their forties, but I swear one didn't look like she should be in a bar.

She was also dancing like a zombie trussed up as a puppet.

It was hilarious and infectious, and soon I was dancing the same. Kennedy bowled over in laughter before she'd go back to a slow grinding motion, and shooting looks at her husband behind her.

I understood.

I knew Caden would be hot for me whenever, and looking at him now, his head was inclined towards Shay as he was speaking, his eyes were firmly on my ass. I gave it a few bounces, and his gaze lifted to mine, surprised.

A slow grin spread over his face, knowing and piercing.

Oh yeah. We'd be hopping on the bed later tonight.

Abruptly the music cut out, and a voice boomed over a microphone. "Ladies and ladies! Gentlemen, too. Are you ready for the extravaganza tonight? It's going to be amazing. It's going to be outstanding. It's going to be life changing! Are. You. Readyyyyyyy for Miss Mermaid Kailaniiiiiiiiiiiiiiiiiiiiiiiiiii?"

The dance techno came back on, but it was heavier, louder, more rocketing through the bar.

Another burst of dry ice filled the bar and a *woosh*. A startled sound came from the other corner of the room, and inside the aquarium was a mermaid.

She was swimming around, dipping, doing rolls. She was doing a whole performance, swimming up, disappearing and then diving back down. Dark pink hair. Rosy cheeks. Dark eyes. Pink eyeliner and a shimmering pink lipstick. She was wearing some kind of velvet bikini top. It could have been because it was in water, but somehow it looked like a deep red velvet, matching her rosy cheeks. And her fin was made of shimmering scales that matched her hair, her lips, and her dark red top. As she continued to flip around the water, which ran the entire length of the other side of the bar, her tail was like a cascade of every color between red and pink, all the different variations.

She was breathtaking.

Then, suddenly, the music cut out and a clip of old school cheers that sounded like they'd been recorded from a basketball game came on. The spotlight swung back to the stage and there were more mermaids there, but they were sitting on chairs and each held a pair of pom poms, the colors all matching their shimmering tails.

They performed a whole cheer along with the music before

the spotlight turned off. The music changed again. Slow. Intense. And it was building, like earlier. Building. Going slow until the spotlight came back on, and it began flashing in rhythm with the music, highlighting different spots through the whole bar. The aquarium, as the mermaid held her own set of pom poms. Back to the stage, the cheerleader mermaids swished their pom poms around in an intricate motion. To the back corner and a new performer was there, but this one was on stilts and standing all the way up into the top corner, half bent over the bar. He looked like a character out of a Tim Burton movie. Then, to the far corner and another person was on stilts over there. As the music sped up, the spotlight matched it, going around and around the room until it was at a dizzying speed, until the very end when the lights flooded the room and all of them began doing a dance in unison.

Hands came to my hips and slid around to the front. The excitement was swirling inside me, but at feeling Caden behind me, I drew in a steadying breath and leaned back, always knowing he'd be a place of shelter for me. I tipped my head up and found him already looking down at me. His eyes were watchful, taking me in as I was taking in the show. He lifted a hand, his finger coming to my bottom lip and as the show continued around us, he dipped, his mouth finding mine.

Another place, another night, I'd be turned around and clambering up in a heartbeat. The ache was there, but I just opened my mouth, his tongue slipped in and I savored the moment. Warm sunlight. That's what he was giving me. We kept kissing for another beat before there was a change in the music. Caden lifted his head, and I glimpsed Kennedy and Shay making out in the corner, her front against his as he was leaning back against the wall by our table. His hands slid into the pockets of her jeans, her arms wound around his neck, but the voice came back over the microphone, drawing my attention to the stage.

A guy was there, rich and long black hair wound around his neck like it was a scarf, and folding down over his chest. He was big, almost as big and muscular as the bartender, but not quite. Dark eyes. Dark lips. He was dressed in pinstripe suit, with dramatic ruffles coming out of the end of his sleeves. He looked like he was in a mermaid tail, too, but was dressed like it was a giant pant, like a sleeve for his legs with matching fabric as his top. He raised a hand up, a microphone in it when suddenly a startled gasp came out of his throat.

His eyes were riveted behind us, and people began noticing, looking as well.

A couple was in the doorway, who looked so striking and matching but in total opposite ways. The beauty of them had everyone pausing in the door, for a millisecond. He was tall, lean, and powerful. Dark blond hair. Sapphire eyes. A full scowl on his face, as he took in the entire bar. There was a darkness that came off him in waves, and as if feeling it, the female next to him glanced his way, a tender slight frown on her face, and she put her palm on his chest. At the touch, he caught her hand, but kept it in place, and lifted his head, his nostrils flared like he was a lion taking a whiff of his future prey. Instead of going on a hunt, he turned his head her way and his eyes softened. The shift was remarkable to watch, but it still sent a shiver down my spine because whoever this guy was, he was dangerous in a killing sort of way.

I leaned fully back against Caden, who was also watching the couple.

Everyone was, even Shay and Kennedy had stopped kissing to notice the change in the club.

The female was still looking at her mate, and it was so obvious they were mates. Or soulmates. My heart pounded against my chest because I had that, what they had. I had that with Caden. Kennedy and Shay had that too. But this couple, it was like they were communicating without words. The beauty of her was also staggering. Dark black hair. A heart-shaped face. Slightly reddened cheeks that were high on her face, frost-bitten green eyes. Her hair grazed over her shoulders, and as if both had come to a conclusion, their heads turned as one. She skimmed a glance over the bar, biting her bottom lip slightly, but the guy flashed a dark glare at the bar, as if the look itself was a command for us to look elsewhere.

And everyone obeyed.

The announcer started back in, his voice slightly trembling before he coughed and got himself under control. A deep boom came next as he gave introductions to the rest of the performing team. We learned each of the cheerleader names, along with the two performers on stilts. Another part of the show was introduced, but I was only half listening.

I was still watching the couple, who had moved to the bar. She was standing back, holding the guy's hand as he was talking to the bartender, our same one, but all the kindness was gone from him. He was leaning forward, everything about him was rigid. He was gripping the counter as if to keep himself from launching over it, and his massive jaw was clenched so tight, I was half worried he was going to break his own teeth.

"What do you think is going on over there?"

Caden looked, drawing me back to the table.

Shay and Kennedy joined us. We weren't the only ones watching the couple. Even the announcer kept looking over as the show continued. A new song came on, but all the performers kept watching them.

Or him.

They were nervous about him.

Shay frowned, pulling Kennedy to stand in front of him and he draped an arm around her front. She held onto him with both her hands.

Gage joined, and Shay asked him, "You know who that is?"

Gage shook his head. He propped his elbow on the table,

leaned against it and stared right at the couple. "Not a clue. A lot of people come in during agate season so they could be a part of that crowd. There does seem to be something different about them, huh?"

One of the local ladies we'd been dancing with joined our group, leaned a heavy elbow in front of Gage, her body turned his way and inclined her head in. "Gum's never got heated with anyone before. We're thinking they're one of his group, if you know what I mean." She gave us all a lingering look, her head dipping down for extra emphasis. Her face was heated and sweaty.

"Who's Gum?" I asked.

Gage asked at the same time, "Gum's got a group?"

She leaned toward me, saying in a way she probably thought she was being discreet, in a way that was not discreet at all, "Gum's the bartender. He's got a weird first name and someone called him Gum because he's always here and working." She blinked once and said to Gage next, "And you know what I'm talking about. They're locals and then there's locals. He's a local local *local*, if you get my drift."

Gage glared. "I have no fucking clue what you're talking about."

She barely shrugged, looking back at Gum, saying at the same time, "Because you're a temp local."

"What does that mean?" he hissed.

She didn't hear him, jumping to attention because she'd finished looking back at Gum, and at the couple, who were staring directly at us. At her. As if they could hear everything she'd just said. She muttered something, making the sign of the cross in front of her before she smacked the table once. "I'm dipping out. See you folks. Nice meeting your hotties." She gave Caden and Shay a wink.

The show had come to an end, but now the announcer guy was over there and words were being exchanged between the guys. Gum had come around to the other side of the bar, and he was standing next to the announcer. The female looked a little upset, but her guy wasn't having it. He stepped forward, getting into the announcer's face. Gum wasn't having *that*, and he stepped forward, his hand raised, and that's when something happened that I couldn't explain.

The couple guy turned towards Gum, his eyes suddenly all dark, and a black something, like dust, lifted off him and swirled around him before lunging for Gum.

Gum was the opposite.

A light blue mist lifted off him, and lunged at the black mist. They collided, and a spark went through the whole bar.

The hairs on the back of my neck stood up. I felt electrified. Everyone felt it, and I jerked towards Caden, who had his serious jawline going, (if you know, you just know), and he moved in front of me. Shay was looking all pissed too, stepping in front of Kennedy.

"What the fuck was that?" Gage took a step away from the table, and then–nothing.

Everyone had been aware something happened, and then everyone was back to normal. A new mermaid was on the stage, and she was dancing. A wave was coming from her, drawing everyone's attention to her. Her movements were mesmerizing. People were stepping away from their tables, enraptured with her. The music ended from the jukebox. She began singing. A low, soothing, but urging tone came from her.

I felt a pounding inside me, a need to–Caden grasped my hand, urging me with him. "Let's get out of here."

Shay had Kennedy in tow, and the guys led us to the back by the bathrooms. There was a door there, and we went through it, out to a parking lot. Once there, I blinked at the sudden lifting of whatever that was going inside that bar. Tension? Pressure? An urging. I had no idea what it was, but it'd been overwhelming.

I turned for Caden, who was pulling me to his side even as I did. He bent his head into my neck, kissed me there and whispered, "You okay?" His hand came up, cradling my neck as he lifted to look at me.

I nodded, having this feeling like we'd just sidestepped a wave of... I had no idea. That was the most unsettling part of it.

Kennedy was leaning into Shay. She was facing us as he was rubbing a hand up and down her back. She frowned. "I have no idea what went on in there, but I also don't want to stick around. Are you guys up for food or something?"

Gage had come with us, a girl with him. Their hands were linked, and he offered, "This is a small town, nothing's open past ten except bars. I've got food at my place that I could warm up." The girl with him was blinking rapidly, as if stunned by the sudden change. She'd been the one he'd been kissing earlier, but she'd not been at the table with us. I had half a thought that maybe he grabbed her as we were leaving and dragged her outside with him. He glanced her way. "Up for food at my place?"

She was still blinking, but nodded. "Yeah. That was...weird in there. Right?" She asked him, "You thought it was weird?"

"It was weird, babe."

Kennedy and I shared a look. Babe?

Maybe she wasn't such a random girl.

He lifted a hand, cupping the side of her face. Her auburn hair fell over his hand and he drew her to him, giving her a light kiss. She seemed more settled after that and was half resting on him for support.

Kennedy shot her eyebrows up at me. *So* not a random girl.

He rested his arm around her shoulders and lifted his chin towards us. "My place it is then."

4

"So." The guys were in the kitchen, drinking beer and standing around while Gage was making whatever he was making. The rest of us were on the patio, and Kennedy said that, leaning back in her seat. "How'd you meet my brother?"

"Uh." The girl's name was Bello, and she reached for her beer, but didn't lift it up from the table. Her fingers rested on the top, and she began picking at the label. Her gaze was focused there. Some of her hair fell forward.

I didn't blame her. Kennedy was making me nervous and I knew her.

Bello laughed, her voice hitching on a note. "I work at the local Safeway. He comes in, a lot."

"I'm sure he does. He's a growing boy."

My eyebrows pulled low. What was Kennedy doing? She was sounding suspicious. Her tone wasn't cold, but it wasn't warm. It wasn't even even. Was she trying to scare the girl away? As long as I'd known Kennedy, her brother never settled down. He was a fuckboy. Kennedy's words, not mine, but I was going to use it. He hadn't wanted to settle down, but we were in our twenties by now. Gage was a year older, so... It made sense he'd eventually find someone and settle down. Bello seemed super nice, so far. She'd not given Kennedy attitude, not once, and we were on hour two of this interrogation. The first hour had been more small talk, chit chat, while Gage could be heard yelling in the kitchen. Apparently the first round of food burned. I blamed the guys for talking and not helping.

I was also hoping to go in and get another fruity drink because Caden knew where the alcohol was. He made me one when we first got here, and I was due for another to keep my buzz. I was in happy puppy mode.

"You know he liked this girl in college, and it didn't end well."

Bello's head jerked back up. "Uh. I didn't know that. We've not talked about that."

"About exes?" Kennedy folded her arms over her chest. "If you're seeing each other, I'd think that's one of the first conversations you have. I mean, lay it all out on the line. Get it over with. You can't keep wasting time, am I right?"

I almost shrunk back in my seat. That'd been the exact reason I even met Caden. Did we really need to bring this topic up?

Kennedy added, "I was used to guys liking me, and then running the other way when they found out who my brothers were in school. That all changed at Dulane, but how about you? Any jerkoff in your past my brother should know about? Any deep emotional damage he or she did to you?"

Bello was biting her bottom lip again. Her beer was in her lap, and she was holding onto it like it was a shield. "Um." She looked my way. Pleading.

Okay. We didn't need to go there. I laughed, forced, and waved my hand in the air. "Exes smexes. Am I right?" I laughed again, another forced note to it, but Bello relaxed. Her shoulders smoothed out, and she gave me a tentative smile.

She said, "Right. Exes smexes."

Kennedy frowned my way. "If you're going to start a relationship, I think you should have everything figured out. It'll make it easier."

"Really? That's how you and Shay got together?"

She started to answer me, then stopped, and closed her mouth. A slight flush came over her cheeks. "There's nothing wrong with being organized, having things figured out."

"Like how?"

She jerked up a shoulder, reaching for her beer. "Making lists. Having a to-do list. Just helps keep your head straight. That's all."

I was fighting back a smile because I knew exactly how she and Shay got together. The star quarterback came up and tossed out all those to-do lists she would've made, and then gave her a good dose of chaos to make her all tingly and happy. And it worked. They had two little boys back home, who Kennedy said her mother was beyond happy to have so they could go on a trip together.

"Look." Bello sighed, putting her beer back on the table. Her hands fell back to her waist. "I really like your brother. I had one boyfriend in my life, from sixth grade through college. After Dutch, I was heartbroken and lost. Your brother's the first guy that I like talking to, who makes me smile when he calls. We're not serious, but I can't handle anything serious."

"You broke up in college?"

Bello didn't answer, her head folding down.

Oh. No. There was a different ending there that maybe Kennedy didn't want to force out the first night she met the girl.

Kennedy's eyebrows were furrowed, sensing something wasn't making sense and she was going to dig in, figure it out, but I jerked forward. And yep. I spilled the drinks on purpose.

Both girls jumped up, and I stood, clasping my hands to my cheeks. "Oh! Look at that." I reached for the glasses before they rolled off. "So clumsy of me. Bello." I saw some had spilled on her lap. "You might want to clean that up?"

She was doing her whole blinking thing again, surprised at the turn of events, but hurried to the patio door. Just as she stepped through to shut it, she paused on the other end and mouthed to me, "Thank you."

I nodded at her before trying to actually clean up the mess with my hands, because I wasn't sure how Gage would react if his patio got stained.

"You did that on purpose."

"Duh." My hands weren't working. I'd need something else.

"I wasn't being that bad."

I stopped, fixing Kennedy with a look. "I don't think she and her ex had a happy ending. That's not for you to force out."

She opened her mouth.

I held up a hand, saying gently, "And I know you weren't reading the signs because otherwise you never would've pushed. Whatever her story is, I think it's a sad one."

The corner of Kennedy's mouth turned down. "Gage really likes her. I can tell. I don't want him to get hurt."

"I know, which is why you're a great sister and you have great brothers." I didn't need to say anything more. Kennedy was a protector. She was protecting her brother, but if circumstances switched, she'd be Bello's protector. She was amazing in that way, and she'd go the extra mile to fight for people she loved by protecting them. I moved to her, forgetting the spill so I could hug her. "It's really great to see you guys again."

She hugged me back. "You too." Her voice came out muffled against my shirt. "But we need to clean this up or Gage will freak over his patio."

I'd been so right in that worry. We both took another second to hug and then got to work wiping all evidence. There was a garbage can around the corner, and Kennedy found paper towels in the garage. When the guys came out, both Caden and Shay paused, taking us in.

Shay cursed first. "Where are your drinks?"

Caden added, "You didn't come back inside, and Gage's girl didn't bring them in either."

Did they know us or did they know us?

Gage was behind them, carrying a tray of pizza slices. He moved around our husbands, putting the tray on the table. "My bad on burning the first round, but these are done to perfection. Slightly burned on the edges..." He trailed off, looking at us, at our guys, and again at us. "What's going on? Bello said she had to go to the bathroom. Is she okay?"

Kennedy smiled brightly, grabbing a slice and taking a bite. "Just hungry, brother. And yum. This is delicious but I need a refill." She hurried inside before he noticed she wasn't carrying a glass.

I held up a finger. "Me too."

Bello came back downstairs as Kennedy was mixing my drink. A pact was made not to tell Gage about the spillage. We were bonded for life now.

5

The first hints of sunrise began when Gage made the suggestion. He stood, yawning, and pointed in the distance. "I live a few blocks from the ocean. Can't tell because the view is blocked by trees, but we could walk there. I know a super secluded beach. Your place is a mile down from there."

We'd stayed up all night. Laughing. Teasing. Reminiscing about our first times hanging out. When Gage met Marcus, Caden's brother. When Kennedy was with me and we ran into Colton at a park, how kind she'd been to him, knowing instinctively to do that because I never told her about him. It was an expressed wish from him, not to tell our friends about him. That was Caden's other brother. There were other stories, but we skipped all the ones about Gage because those usually included a girl of the week, and we were being respectful to Bello, who had curled up in Gage's lap, drowsing off until he just now stood.

She stood with him, rubbing at her eyes, and giving in to a full yawn. She reached out for his hand and waved with her other one to everyone. "Think I'm going to pass. I have a shift later, need to sleep. It was really nice meeting everyone."

Hugs were given. Kennedy said she was happy to have met her, and she sounded genuine.

She told me later, as we were heading down a path in the woods, linking elbows, "I think she's the only girl I've really felt okay about with Gage. He liked a friend of mine in college, but it didn't work out. I like Bello." A small crease formed between her eyebrows, and knowing Kennedy, she was wondering what her sad story about the ex was.

I covered her hand with mine. "When she's ready to tell, she will. I bet Gage already knows."

"Why do you think that?"

I shrugged, thinking back and remembered the small touches he gave her. How he touched her back, her elbow, held her hand, rubbed her when she was on his lap. "Just a feeling. He seemed protective, a bit."

"Well, as long as he knows."

And that was Kennedy being a good sister. I would've loved to have her as a sister.

The guys were ahead of us, but both Shay and Caden glanced back to check on us. I beamed at Caden, and he grinned back. It was getting that time where I was missing my husband. I liked, no, I *loved* spending time with great friends, but I could only go so long without having the hubby time.

Once we got to the beach, climbing through two giant boulders, Caden was there, waiting for me. He took my hand. It was almost rehearsed because without a second thought, Kennedy detached and reached for Shay, who was reaching back for her too.

We could hear the waves, and barely see them because the sun had just started to rise, but it was a beautiful sight. Gage was right, we had our own private beach—or no.

A shout of laughter rang out, just around the last boulder. Gage was already there and was frozen.

I rounded it, trying to see, but as soon as I did, Caden yanked me back.

"But–" His hand clamped over my mouth and I got why a second later, as I inched forward, but still hidden around the boulder, what I was seeing finally clicked into understanding it.

It was the mermaids from the show, from the bar, but they weren't in costume this time. They were standing on the beach, with two legs. Okay. Yeah. Mermaids weren't real. I got it, but it was fun to pretend for a night. Plus, the twerking. That was super fun too. A whole group was together, and yep... they were naked. A full skinny-dipping event. That's what was going to happen.

I was looking for Gum, but he wasn't with them.

They lined up, some were laughing. Some weren't. Some were almost sullen, or bored. Then, the announcer guy joined and whoa, he was ripped. I must've made a sound, because Caden snorted a choked laugh in my ear. He was fully pressed over me, also looking. I looked, saw that Gage had been pulled back. I was hoping he was still hidden from their view. I mean, they were just skinny dipping, and it was a normal thing to do. Or maybe? I'd only skinny dipped with Caden and that led to something else really quick, and right on cue, a fresh, but yummy shiver wound through my body because as soon as we were alone, I'd be down for doing that again.

But back to the nude beach goers, we shouldn't be spying.

I was starting to feel bad, and began to pull back when suddenly, as one being, they all started a mad dash into the ocean.

That was fun. I was smiling with them, but then–no. What? I gasped, because they went in and when they emerged from the waves, they dove back in but what flipped out after them wasn't legs.

It was a tail. From all of them.

There were about twelve of them total, a total of twelve tails doing the whole mermaid flip that you see in the movies, and I was seeing it in real life.

What. The. *Mermaids*?

I was expecting them to come back, emerge, and they'd be carrying a fake mermaid tail with them. They'd be laughing about it because it was a prank, but no. They never emerged. After they did one or two tail flips, they were gone.

I had a feeling they'd emerge again for their next mermaid show in the bar.

I was light-headed, making a realization that I would've been squealing about if I were a little girl still. Mermaids were real. Holy–

"And they wanted me to find you, wipe your memories because of what *I* did last night."

It was the couple from the bar, the guy and his girlfriend, who, man, she was so pretty. Her hair was swept up in a messy bun, with long tendrils flowing around her face. Wearing a sarong dress, she looked like something out of a fairytale. The guy, he could've been the villain.

Last night he came off as mildly irritated. This morning, he was smug and sporting a smirk.

"You can keep it moving." Caden stepped in front of me.

"No need to get into something here." Shay had done the same thing with Kennedy, who shot me a look, and I got it because oh my God, what was happening here?

"Kellan," the girl murmured. "Don't play with them. Just get it done and let's have our beach day."

He shot her an amused look. "Haven't we learned from the one Christmas? I need to indulge my demon side–"

"Demon?" I squawked. Mermaids. Now demons? Was the girl a demon too?

The girl sighed. "There you go. Playing again. These are humans. They're meant to be protected."

He snorted. "Says your Messenger side. That's not my base, Shay."

"Shay?" Kennedy squawked now, stepped around her Shay and looking between the two.

"Now they know our names. We really do need to wipe their memories." The guy was back to being amused.

She Shay sighed, again. She turned and addressed us, "This is nothing personal. You guys are the only ones who left the bar before we could make you forget what you saw."

"What'd we see?" Caden asked, his tone low and deadly.

A puff of pride bloomed in my chest. My man. Taking on a demon. Though, how dangerous was this demon? And I still couldn't believe I was thinking about a demon in real life here. Not fantasy or the dark romance paranormal kind. I was pushing down my fear because if I indulged, I'd be doing something embarrassing. Like pissing myself. Or worse, and I didn't want to go there.

"You saw a territorial interaction. The local Mers didn't want Kellan and I to be vacationing here, but that's all. And now, he's going to wipe your memories and all will be good again." There was an extra light beaming around her eyes, in the iris. And as she spoke, it glowed brighter, sending a warmth coating us. Coating me. I suddenly wanted to close my eyes and give in, but give in to what? I didn't know. I just wanted to do it. It was similar to the feeling last night when the one performer mermaid began singing.

Wiping our memory. That's what was going to happen.

"Wait." I stuck my hand up in the air.

The warmth ceased, and the Kellan guy began chuckling before his girl smacked his arm. He cut it off as she asked, "You don't have to raise your hand here."

"Oh." I looked at my hand, confused myself about why I'd done it. Then I shrugged. "If you're going to wipe our memories, what will you put in its place?"

"What do you mean?" The Kellan guy's head had tilted at his question.

I shrugged, before glancing around. "I don't know. I mean, we had a great night. I enjoyed the bar, the show, and seeing my friends? It was a night I'd like to remember. We laughed. Kennedy interrogated her brother's new girlfriend–"

"She did what?" from Gage.

"I just love you, that's all."

"–we stayed up all night, telling stories before we came down here. Gage burned the first round of pizzas, which took a whole hour so that made sense that he'd burned them. He took too long."

Kennedy added, "Way too long."

"Hey. You interrogated Bello."

"—The night was beautiful, and I don't want to forget any part of it. Not one bit." I ignored the siblings, staring hard at She Shay.

She shared a look with her man before she gave a nod, stepping forward to me. "We're going to replace the memories of what you saw in the bar." As she began speaking, there was a wave coming from her man. Her Kellan. He wasn't saying anything, but I knew somehow, they were working in conjunction together. She was laying the groundwork, and he was doing the erasing.

She came closer to me, touching my temples with her fingers, and her voice dropped to a crooning whisper, but it was the emotions I was feeling from her. They were beautiful, and warm, and loving, and it was something else I didn't want to forget either. I didn't know what she was, but I didn't care at the moment. It was breathtaking.

Maybe we should've fought more? Maybe the guys could've threatened them, but the truth is that the whole night was surreal. It was like a page taken out of a storybook, and there was a part of me that almost didn't believe any of this was happening. These were supernatural creatures. We as humans weren't supposed to have witnessed them, known they existed. They were powerful and dangerous, so maybe wiping our memories was what needed to be done?

She kept murmuring, a song-like lyrical note joining with her voice, "You will remember everything until the moment you saw myself and Kellan. You will not remember anything about us except that we were there, and we sat at a table in the corner. We enjoyed the show with everyone else. You will remember everything after that point until you came down to this beach. Instead of seeing the Mer tails, you instead saw a group of friends going for a swim. You saw them rejoin on the beach, walking on two legs, and once they picked up their clothes and left, you and your friends continued on your walk of the beach. You will remember this night as a blessed night, a precious memory, and you'll rethink on this night with loving fondness because as you said, it's a night to be remembered. You will not remember Kellan and myself finding you on this beach. You will not remember anything we've spoken about here. With time, the memory of us being a normal couple enjoying the show in the bar with you will also fade. And now as your memories are taken, I fill in the gentle openings with laughter, love, and kindness. The magic will give us a pocket of time where we will leave, and once we are out of ear and eyesight, everything will be complete."

Everything she said happened.

Until it didn't.

6

"Are you kidding me?" A sudden growl came from behind us. It was Gum, but he didn't look like the Gum we saw in the bar earlier. This Gum had his hair loose, and it was flowing freely around his face, and his eyes were lit and furious. His massive jawline was tense. And he was wearing a muscle tank, which showed how very large and muscular his muscles were. He looked like a body builder's wet dream except without the veins sticking out. Kinda like a mix between Thor and the Hulk guy, when he was in the green mode. And he was wearing loose cloth pants that were half ripped so they were flowing around his legs, just like his hair. Barefoot too.

She Shay cut off, right before there was another growl from her guy, who stepped forward. "We're doing what we were asked. This is me being nice. Do not make me want to be un-nice."

She Shay cast her guy a nervous look, but Gum snapped back, "Lancaster had no authority to ask you to do this to these humans. They're under Arogyous's protection."

Well, that changed everything.

Who was Arogyous?

At the name, the Demon guy stopped being all growly and there was a lifting in the air. It took three seconds, but the rest of my friends began looking around in confusion and panic.

She Shay raised her hand, the same crooning tone coming from her. "Calm. No one is in danger here."

They calmed. The girl had serious power.

Demon guy said, still a little growly, "I wasn't told Arogyous was here."

"Who's Arogyous?" Caden asked.

I harrumphed because *exactly*.

She Shay, Demon Guy, and Gum all ignored him.

I answered, "No clue, but apparently we're under his protection. And there's a Lancaster dude who wanted our memories wiped, but he had no authority to ask for that."

"What?" Kennedy's mouth was on the sand. Her Shay stepped over, pulling her into his arms.

Gage was still shaking his head. "I'm so confused by what's going on. Did you see those people? And they went into the ocean?" He faced the ocean, his legs unsteady. "They never came back. And what was that? You think a giant goldfish ate them?"

She Shay said to Demon Guy, "I don't think you need to wipe *his* memories."

"Enough." Gum's voice rose. "Arogyous said they could stay at his place. That means they're under his protection. It's his call what happens to them."

The Demon guy's eyes went dark again. "I do not adhere under the control of Aimilios Arogyous. You're forgetting who you're talking to."

Gum seemed to waver for the first time, his head lowering a little, as well as his tone. "I do not forget who you are, Kellan, and whose son you are. But Aimilios is my best friend, and wiping the memories of humans under his protection is something he doesn't agree with."

Kellan took a step closer to Gum, his head tilting, and a shiver went down my spine because I had the distinct feeling he was considering just killing Gum. He said, his voice soft, but it sent waves of fear through me, "Are you forgetting your own blood's calling? Do you think I don't know who you are, Prin–"

"Enough." The word whipped out of Gum, but he took a shaking step back. "Who my family is has no say here either."

Kellan continued to study him, until his Shay stepped to him. Her hand went to his arm. She spoke to Gum, "We don't care if these human's memories are wiped or not. Your man Lancaster insisted it be done, for their sake. We agreed it would more helpful to them if they forgot what they saw happened earlier. They must not have understood it, but later, it could trigger them to start trying to understand."

Kellan shot her a look.

She amended, "I agreed it would be more helpful to them."

Oooh! Ooh! I shot my hand up.

No one paid attention to me.

I waved it. "Me! I have something to say."

She Shay frowned, her eyebrows pulling low together. "Did you wipe my memories, Kellan? Did I already say we don't need to raise hands here."

He just chuckled, his eyes gleaming with some evil amusement.

I dropped my hand as Caden rubbed my back. "Can I just say that what we saw in the bar is nothing compared to this whole experience, and also, my memory wasn't wiped." I gestured to my friends. "I could tell when you lifted it from them, how they clued in, but me–I'd known the whole time what was going on."

That drew Kellan's attention. His gaze sharpened on me, and he started for me, but his woman grabbed his hand, keeping him beside her. I felt a pulsing power blast me, and almost fell over from it. Caden readied me, snarling at Kellan, "Stop it."

The power stopped, and Kellan chuckled, dryly. "Or what? You're human."

Caden's gaze darkened, and our Shay took a step closer to the couple.

Kellan noticed, but only drew a breath as his Shay's hand touched his chest. She moved in front of him. She spoke to us, "We have no wish to harm humans, but make no mistake that he is more demon than human. Do not provoke him. We've had instances where his demon side broke apart from his human side, and it was not pretty. I don't say this to scare you. I say this to help you remember we're not all like you. You don't know our world or our rules. Caution would be wise."

"He has rules to follow?" Shay asked.

Gum snorted. "No. He's probably the only being who doesn't, but he's chosen to live here because of her."

Kellan gave him a piercing look.

Gum's eyebrows rose. "Yeah, man. Even I heard about the Son of the Dark Lord, who walks the world because he fell in love with a Messenger."

"You show respect now?"

Gum snorted again. "It's not respect, dumbass. It's called knowing who the big baddies are, which is smart for me to do."

"If you know who I am, you know I don't need to adhere to your friend's claim of protection."

"But you will." Gum gave an easy nod towards She Shay. "Because she cares, and because you love her. What are you even doing here? I never got a real answer before Lancaster showed up, issuing threats back at the bar."

"We're on vacation," she answered. "We graduated college, and we're taking a year before I start graduate school."

"You? College?"

Kellan began chuckling.

"It's more me, and yes. Education is always a good idea." She gave him a onceover. "You never went to college? You look as if you could house an entire fraternity, just yourself."

Gum's amusement was evident in his crooked grin. "I went. And yeah, I joined a fraternity. It's fun being a human sometimes."

Okay. Lovely. They were bonding over pretending to be us. I started to raise my hand, but jerked it back down. "I have a question." And before I even got a look, I said it. "How come we're under this Aimilios guy's protection?"

"I already said. You're staying at his place."

"We're under his protection just because of that? He doesn't know us. That's it?"

Gum shrugged. "You've got a look to you. I knew some of the Mers might want to mess with you, so I messaged my friend. His power was cast over you as soon as he said you could stay at his place, and because of that, the Mers stayed away from you."

Caden growled. "What do you mean they would've tried to mess with her?"

"You know. Same reason you were drawn to her. There's something off with her, but it draws a person in. Supernatural creatures are just as drawn as humans are to her. I did you a favor."

Caden spat out, "Did you really?"

Gage decided to join the conversation, raking a hand through his hair. "I have no idea what's going on, but I'm heading back to check on Bello. Also, I'm tired. I don't want to go in the ocean anymore. I think that giant goldfish is still out there."

"We're going to go, too." Shay shared a look with Caden, skimming over the Supernaturals. His hand guided Kennedy ahead of him, as she began to follow her brother. "We'll talk later?"

Caden nodded. "Try to sleep."

Shay grunted under his breath. "Got no idea how that's going to go, but I'm thinking we need a debrief drink later today."

Nothing else was said as the three left.

Caden asked once they were out of sight, "You're not going to do anything to us?"

Kellan's eyes took on another evil gleam, and his top lip lifted in a sneer, but his woman said, her hand firmly pressing on his chest, "No. We're not here to upset any treaty already in place, and we know other humans who are aware of us. We'd only do something if you asked."

I had a feeling it wouldn't work on me, but I wasn't going to say that. Maybe I was just special? But the evil guy had reacted when he found out his powers hadn't worked on me, and I did not want to endure that again. He seemed to have let it go.

Also, I was *so* just going with the fact that I was special. Made sense to me.

Caden's hand pressed on my back. "Then we're going to go. Apparently we have a mile to walk."

"Nah. I'll give you a ride." Gum motioned into the trees. "My Jeep is parked a little ways away. I can show you how to get inside Aimilios's place."

Caden and I didn't move.

Gum flashed a blinding smile and he looked like a surfer in that moment. "I just fought for you. Got no plans to undo all of that. It's not the funnest taking on this guy, if you get my drift." He gestured towards Kellan, who was now back to looking bored. He had pulled his woman into his arms, waiting for whatever she wanted to do. One of his arms was wrapped around her shoulders, in front of her neck. She relaxed back into him.

Caden glanced my way.

I shrugged. I had no problems with Gum. I had no problems with She Shay either, but Kellan was different. He had a wild and unpredictable feel to him. *I* liked being the unpredictable one. My hand found Caden's and I said, "That's fine with me."

We followed Gum, but only after he shared a heated look with the couple.

His Jeep was parked on the side of a road, and once we got in, it hit me. "Jason Momoa."

"Huh?"

"That's who you look like. I had it wrong. You're like a blond fraternity version of Jason Momoa."

Yes. That was such a better description, and now I was happy. I figured it out.

7

W e went to get our camper truck first, then followed
Gum to the hotel.

The boutique hotel was better in person. It was like a giant house, that also looked like a mini castle. There was one side that was a tower, complete with the pointed roof. If I'd seen this place on YouTube, or on the internet, I would've wanted to stay here anyways. I was almost salivating.

Gum drove into the large parking lot, he veered to the left of the place, towards the tower, and away from the front entryway. A small gravel roadway broke off from the parking lot and then around the tower. He went that route. On the other side, a whole building extended out towards the ocean.

He kept going, pulling into a small parking slot, and cut the engine.

We pulled in behind him, and as we got out, he motioned to the extended building, and said, "This is where my buddy stays. He uses it when he's in town." He indicated towards the entry area. "Don't even go over to the other side, because it's run by a rental management. They won't have any idea who you're talking about if you mention my buddy, or myself. Well, they might know me. Mermaid Bar is frequented by all the locals, and well, I guess they do know I'm friendly with the owner. But that's it. They don't know anything else."

Caden opened our camper and he and Gum reached in, pulling out our bags. Gum grabbed everything within reach, piling it high so he was carrying twelve bags. That vision itself should've been a dead giveaway he wasn't just human. Caden gave him a look before shaking his head.

I peeked inside, but everything had been grabbed. Oh, not my pillow. I grabbed that and hugged it to my chest, because… well, just because.

We followed him down to a door, and he put in a code. The door slid open, and as we stepped inside, lights turned on. The place was modern on the inside. A large dark gray sectional sat in the middle of the room. A kitchen on one end, with an island that had a waterfall gradient. Stainless steel appliances. The refrigerator was translucent, and completely empty. Gum hit a switch and all the window shades opened, sliding up. A giant television was mounted high on the wall, before the sectional. There was also a gaming area with a pool table, foosball, air hockey, Skee-Ball, and a dart machine.

The place was high end and masculine.

Gum headed to the right, and started up the stairs. "I'll drop your stuff off up here. My bud won't want you to use his bedroom, so I'll put these in the room that'll be cool."

He wasn't gone long, within seconds, and he talked the whole way. His voice was clearer as he jogged back down. "Stay off the third floor. That's his area. Anywhere on the second floor is cool to use. He's got an office up there for guests to use, a library, you'll see. And of course, down here is cool." He went to the kitchen area and pushed a button. A large door began opening, bringing an entire giant-sized box that extended from the ceiling to the roof. Once it was all the way out, Gum motioned to a set of dials. "This shit isn't known yet, but he's got a robot-cooking station in here. And knowing my buddy, it's all stocked up. It'll ask what you want, and you can type it in, see if it'll make it for you. When I want to live in the lap of luxury, I'll bring a date over here sometimes." He winked at us. "Don't tell my bud. Though, he's got cameras outside and on the main floor. None in the bedrooms or bathrooms. He could find out if he cared, and thankfully for my dates, he never cares." A goofy grin appeared as he came back to where we were still rooted in place.

He cocked his head to the side. "You guys good?" The lines around his mouth crinkled. "Guess you kinda have a lot to process, huh?"

"What are you?" Caden asked.

"I'm–uh–that's not important, and really, do you need more information to process?"

"Are there really mermaids, demons, and messengers? Also, what's a messenger?"

He opened his mouth to answer, then thought better of it and closed it with a smile. "You know, while I don't think wiping memories is cool, I gotta admit that maybe the less you know, the better. Messes with your head *more*, you know." He lifted up his shoulder. "Okay then. I'm out. The code to get in and out is on the board by the door. It changes every time you enter the place, so make sure to look at the new one to get back inside. It's a whole automatic security thing." He gave another wave heading back. "Hope you have a great rest of your adventure." The door slid open for him, and shut once he cleared the doorway.

We heard his jeep pulling away a little later.

Caden turned to look at me. "Holy fuck."

He spoke for both of us.

8

————

"You doing okay?" Caden touched my stomach, his hand sliding up under my tank and cupping one of my breasts. His thumb rubbed over my nipple, slow and purposeful. We'd laid down for a nap. It was too late in the morning to go to *sleep* sleep for us, and since I didn't want to totally mess up our sleep schedule, a nap it was.

Glancing at the clock, I saw that was six hours ago.

There went that idea.

I rolled towards him, and moved my leg between his, reaching to hug him. Caden helped pull me over so I was half laying on him. I nestled down in the crook of his shoulder, and his hand reached up to smooth down my hair, my back, sliding to my ass before coming back up to my stomach. I loved when he did that.

I yawned, getting more comfortable, and not wanting to wake up. "I'm okay, considering everything this morning." I was ignoring what happened last night because there was no comparison to this morning. That was the real mind-blowing event. "Mermaids are real. Holy shit, Caden."

He chuckled, his voice low and a little gritty from sleep, and rubbed his hand over my back. "And demons and whatever that girl was."

"Shay. She has the same name as our Shay."

His phone began ringing, and grabbing it, he showed me the screen. *Shay calling.*

I didn't think it was the girl version.

He answered it and put it on speaker as I sat up, drawing my knees to my chest. "What's up?"

Shay snorted from his end. "My dick. All night."

Caden grinned. "Kennedy wound up?"

"She's writing lists, and then she's writing lists of those lists. She thinks if she can organize all this new madness, that she'll feel better." He sighed. "I have a conditioned response to when she starts getting all Organized Kennedy. I want to fuck it out of her, so yeah. I've been hard all day. How are you guys doing? How are the digs?"

Caden yawned as he answered, "They're nice. Real futuristic and shit. Also, you're on speaker."

"Aw. Fuck. Hi, Summer."

I leaned towards the phone. "Kennedy's aware of your conditioned response to her getting uptight?"

He laughed. "Fuck yeah. It's why we got together."

I smiled. "Piss her off."

"I'm planning on it right after finding out if you guys are sticking around or heading out?"

Caden and I shared a look. He raised his eyebrows. "I'm good for sticking around. We don't have a set plan, and we have friends here. When are you guys leaving?"

"Kennedy wants to stay and see more of her brother. We don't see him that often."

Caden asked me, "You good with that?"

I gestured around the room. "We weren't told how long we could stay here, but the way Gum was talking, his friend wasn't coming back anytime soon. We could stop by Mermaid Bar, see if he's working? Run it by him, just to be safe."

"If he says no, Gage said you could pull park your truck here. That'd kinda be fun."

Caden's smile flashed. "I don't think you heard the important part that Summer said." He sat up, holding the phone and his stomach flexed, all his nice tattoos shifting from the movement. "She wants to go back to the bar."

Shay caught on. "Drinking."

"Day drinking."

"Fuck. Let's pretend we're in college again."

Caden gave me a wolfish grin as we finalized the details of when to meet up. Shay had a plan to go and 'piss off' Kennedy, preferably in the shower, and catching how Caden was looking at me, I was thinking he had similar intent.

I started to rise up from the bed, but he caught me, lifting me fully in the air. "Caden!" But my body was already responding. And as he carried me to the bathroom, the shower turned on, and within a moment, my back was pushed up against the wall.

I loved my husband. And I really loved how this need for him only got grew with every day.

I was panting by the time he lifted me up, growling, and then he thrust inside.

No matter what we found out today, nothing else mattered except him and I, and our family. Then I stopped thinking, and began pushing back against him because let's make this fucking hot *and* fun today.

9

Gum was behind the bar as we walked in, and he paused in pouring a drink, one of his eyebrows lifting up. "Humans."

I braked abruptly because there were two people sitting in front of him, but neither moved a muscle. Their backs were to us.

A big smile spread over Gum's face and he set his bottle back down. He didn't seem bothered by their presence. "Welcome." That eyebrow wiggled. "You guys just had to come in and see the Gumster, didn't you? I made an impression. It's okay. I have adoring fans all over the seas."

Caden asked, his tone dry, "That you telling us you're a Mer guy?"

"Fuck no. I'm just telling you I have fans all over the seas. They all love me. Humans and Mers."

Kennedy walked around us, giving Gum a cautious look. "Odd jokes aside, do you have food?"

And as if on command, my stomach let loose with a loud rumble.

Everyone heard. Everyone looked, even the two guys at the

bar. Their eyes were glazed over so I was figuring they were too drunk to make sense of anything. But well, I guess they heard my tummy and Caden laughed, stepping to me, his hand going there as if to settle my hunger down. "I've not done my job today. She's not eaten yet."

Gum just flashed another smile and grabbed a couple menus, handing it over. "You up for drinks too?"

"I'll have what I had last night."

Kennedy added, "Not me. I want wine, and I'm not a wine snob. I'll take whatever is cheapest."

Caden gestured to Shay. "We'll do what's local and on tap for beer, your choice."

"Really?"

Shay flashed him a grin. "We're going to try and drink like we're still in college. Should get interesting."

"Noted." Gum jerked up his chin as we moved to a table in the corner. It was a lower one, not a high top, and I felt a little more grounded knowing I wasn't going to fall off my stool. Considering everything, I wasn't feeling the most settled.

"Humans we know."

The demon guy, Kellan, was making his way towards us. His hair was ruffled and messy. He had a sleepy smirk on his face, but as he took the seat next to Shay, his gaze skimmed over all of us. Those eyes were not sleepy. They were alert, and dark.

A nervous sensation buzzed through me, and I sat up straighter. Kennedy's gaze was locked on him, her jaw tight. "Are you here to issue us more threats?"

He frowned at her, grabbing for a menu as his woman approached us and after a second's hesitation, took the seat next to me. She gave me a friendly grin, but it was a little wary.

He asked Kennedy, "Did I threaten you?"

"You were going to wipe our memories."

"That wasn't a threat. I was just going to do it."

"Oh my–Kellan, stop playing with her."

Our Shay growled under his breath. "I don't know who I need to meet to find out how to seriously hurt you, but I will. Stop fucking with us, and especially my wife."

Kellan's nostrils flared. "Wife? You guys seem too young to be married. How old are you?"

I leaned forward. "Uh. We don't need to go over that, but we've been married, been out of college, and have children. That'll give you an idea."

"Yeah." Kennedy shot me a grin.

I laughed and then asked, because when else would I ever have a demon sitting at my table and I'd know about it? "How old are you guys?"

"We're–" She Shay spoke up, her voice rising and shooting her man look so he knew she'd be handling the questions from now on. "We graduated last year and we're taking a gap year before I start graduate school."

"Oh." Fun! "What are you going for?"

"Shay wants to save the world."

She shot him another aghast look. "I'm going for social work. I want to work in administration and go as high as I can."

Gum came over, bringing all of our drinks, setting them on the table. He gave us all a lingering gaze before turning to leave. "This is an interesting bunch considering."

Kellan said, deadpanning while he reached for his drink, "I've already been threatened once and told to be quiet."

Gum paused, scrutinizing him for a beat. "I'd assumed you'd get threatened a lot more than that."

"Day's early. Only been here for a few minutes. Ask again in thirty."

Gum snorted a laugh, his head shaking, and he slipped back behind the bar.

"What are you?" Caden's voice drew the attention of everyone at our table. He asked She Shay, but there was no judgment or expression on his face. The question was genuine. "I—just want to know what we're dealing with here."

She hesitated, and shared a look with her man, but he was quiet. "My father was an angel. We call them messengers."

"Oh!" I looked between the two. "An angel and a demon?"

"I'm only half."

"What's your other half?" That came from Our Shay.

"Human." She shared another look with Kellan, this time more lingering.

How did that work? An angel and a demon? But it must've because it was obvious he was head over heels for her. I frowned. "How did you meet? Like was it a scene where it was a battle to the death? You're enemies. Then you meet and *bam*, the first time your sword slices into her, you're suddenly wishing a different sword was going–"

"Summer." Kennedy was laughing. "Oh my God."

She Shay's eyes gentled. "It wasn't like that, but now I'm kinda wishing it were. A more interesting story than what did happen." They were doing the 'look' thing and they were so having their own conversation.

"Enough about us. What are you all doing here? And what are your names?"

We told her, which she got a kick out of the shared Shay name. Kellan just kept giving Our Shay odd looks for a while until we'd ordered our third round, and ate through three pizzas.

Kellan left the table at one point, and it wasn't soon after when we had another round of drinks and food coming to our table. If he'd ordered them, it would've taken longer to get here because Mermaid Bar had filled with more customers since we'd first come in.

I was going with my theory that he used his magic powers for us. When it came to pizza and drinks, I was down for it.

10

———————

I was winded, and I couldn't believe I was saying that. But I was. A DJ came in, and we'd been dancing for the last three hours straight. I had sweat sliding down my back, and had no idea how my hair was looking. And when I said we were dancing, I meant Kennedy, myself, and She Shay. Also, She Shay was awesome at dancing. She could twerk way better than me and Kennedy. I was blaming her magic powers for that because if I'd had to choose any magic powers, twerking would be it. Or flying.

Probably twerking, but I needed a break.

Heading back to the table, I saw only Kellan sitting there. He had a whole steely gaze going on, and he switched from watching his woman shaking it to watching me coming toward him. When I got there, I sat on the chair across from him and looked around.

"Your man is trying to pay the bill. The male Shay went to piss."

Male Shay. I liked He Shay better. Or Our Shay. I wiped at some sweat on my forehead. "Oh. Cool."

He'd gone back to watching his Shay, but his gaze flitted to me once again. "Cool? That's what you human folk say nowadays?"

I considered it and shrugged. "Pretty sure it's supposed to be 'lit' now. I'm showing my age. I think 'awesome' shows it more."

"Words are so fickle. They have power that humans don't respect."

I frowned. "I respect my words. I don't say anything that'll hurt someone unless it's the truth and it's supposed to help in the long run. I have a feeling you don't have the same regards."

"I'm a demon. What are you not getting about that?"

I shrugged, relaxing more into my seat. "A demon lost over his angel. Love kinda screwed you."

His eyes sharpened. "Excuse me?"

"I mean, look at you. All brooding and badass. Your whole aura is like 'don't mess with me or I'll squash you with a thought.'"

He leaned forward, a dangerous smile starting to form. "I *can* squash you with a thought. Don't tempt me, Human."

Okay. Now I was getting irritated. The back of my neck was heated up and angry. "Stop calling me that name."

He frowned, a flicker. "You are a human."

"Do you want me to refer to you as Demon? Yes, Demon. No, Demon. Whatever you say, Demon. I'd think it would get annoying."

That evil grin was back. "I prefer it. Thank you."

I flushed. "My name is Summer. Yours is Kellan."

There was a twitch in his gaze, and I swear that it was amusement. He was enjoying this conversation. I narrowed my eyes, sitting back, giving him a longer studying look. "You know what I think?"

"I have a feeling I won't have to wait long to find out."

"I think you're so in love with Shay, and she's having so much fun, that not only are you doing this to appease her, *you're* also kinda having fun too. I'm right. Aren't I?"

A flicker of annoyance blazed from him briefly. "I want to kill most humans. I only half want to murder you. Satisfied?"

I was. Immensely.

I beamed back at him. "I have that effect on people. I grow on them like weird seaweed." A different thought came to me. "Do you see spirit animals?"

A bored expression was starting to settle over him before my last question. He frowned again. "What?"

"Spirit animals. Do you see them? I've always thought I have a bee as mine. Do I? Can you confirm that?"

He looked around me before shaking his head. "Why do you think you have a bee?"

I was so right. "I do, don't I? You can just confirm it and we'll move in. Promise."

He sighed. "You have an entire hive around you."

My chest puffed up. Even better. A hive sounded better than just one bee. And I was remembering the earlier conversation. "Wait. If Shay is going to grad school, what are you doing to do? Did you go to college with her?"

His eyes burned at me. "I can have your mouth disappear. You'd stop asking me questions."

On the fear scale, he was all the way at the top, but my gut was telling me that I was safe. I leaned forward again, folding my arms and resting them on the table. "Did you? Go to college? What's your degree? Do you have to do normal jobs for money or do you magically woosh money up for you? Are you rich?"

"Woosh?"

I made a motion with my hand. "You know. Magic. Poof, there's a pile of money for you."

His gaze turned cold, but he said, stiffly, "My father runs the underworld. I have money."

Oh. Ooh. New fear trickled through me. "Like Lucifer?"

"Do you really want me to confirm that?"

Oh boy. Maybe I needed to learn to think before I launched an interrogation, but no... His woman was all good, and he said he only wanted to half murder me. I had a feeling that spoke volumes for him. My shoulders loosened back up. "But what about college? Were you like this? Reluctantly participating so your girlfriend–"

"She's not my girlfriend. She's my soulmate."

The speed he corrected me almost gave me whiplash. It was so fast. And I was impressed. "You really do love her."

He glowered at me. "I didn't care about college, but Shay did. So I participated, and my professors did what I wanted them to do."

I knew it! "You used your magic powers to get good grades. I'd *so* do that if I could, and I wouldn't feel guilty about it."

He shook his head slightly. "You're the type of seaweed that grows on creatures until it slowly suffocates them and kills its host. Then you eat it for nourishment."

I grinned. I was pretty sure that was a compliment from him. "Thanks."

11

———

The night was great. Also, I was a little buzzed.

Also, I was hungry.

Also, I loved Caden so much. I mean, holy freaking snake-tattoo-on-the-arm Batman. I wanted to take him home, strip off his clothes, do a sexy dance for him, climb up and show him my version of what a ride in the Bat mobile must be like. Who wouldn't?

Okay. I might've been drunk, but the night was great. So much dancing. Laughs. Shay and Kellan were cute to watch together. He'd scowl. She'd smile at him, and bam, the glower would lift to blankness. For him, that was love.

I was starting to understand him. Maybe...

But now it was closing, and we were the last couples in the bar. I had enough energy to go to an after party, and that was such a college thing to do. I decided to announce it to the group. "Hey guys–"

The door burst open with a slam, which was impressive because Gum had just ushered the last of his staff out. He locked the door, and turned to head back to do whatever else he needed. I wasn't sure why he hadn't kicked us out yet, maybe sentimentality? He had a soft spot for us, but I was doubting it. It was more likely that he was scared of me. Not Kellan. Me. Who'd blame him? I could be ferocious.

"Excuse me?" Gum turned right around, and seemed to double in size.

I rubbed at my eyes, because that couldn't be true. Right?

I caught a glimpse of the demon and angel next to me, and remembered what world I now knew about.

"Excuse you," the last word was spat as the door shut again, and Lancaster walked around Gum. His eyes were bulging, and he also seemed to have doubled in size from the night before. Red rings surrounded his irises as he took us in. "Humans cannot be allowed to know who we are. Their minds must be wiped clean." He jerked his head to Kellan. "You have failed, Son of–"

"If you say my father's name, I will kill you."

God.

Kellan said that so casual, like he had better things to do right now. Like getting a manicure. But when he lifted his head, his eyes were anything but casual. A new wave of awareness filled the room, settling over all of us, and the hairs on the back of my neck stood up.

"You would dare threaten me? I am Lancaster of the–"

"I'm aware of who you are. It's you who is forgetting their place."

A darkness came off Kellan, a literal wave of darkness. It swirled around him, from feet to toes, and it grew, filling the room as he spoke.

"Kellan." Shay reached out, touching his arm. Her voice was soft.

As she spoke, some of the darkness dissipated, but not all of it. It was still swirling around him, hanging tight at the moment.

She took a step forward. "I remember you from last night,

Mr. Lancaster, but I don't believe we exchanged our own names."

"Because he makes the mistakes so many others do." Kellan smirked at him. "He's thinks I'm the only threat in here."

Gum grunted.

Shay shot Gum a small smile, who'd returned to his normal buff size. "We're aware of your affiliations."

"Thank you. That's all I wanted to add." He held out a hand, moving back to the counter. "Have at it, but if you break anything you're fixing it. Also, you have until I finish my work before everyone is out. And I mean it. Everyone. I don't give a damn what the issue is here."

"Tor–"

As he spoke, Gum returned to his doubled size, and his voice thundered out of him, "You will not say my name." The room shook. The tables. Glassware fell, shattering. The floorboards began shaking underneath us. "You forgot the territory you're in, Lancaster of the Roku Family. I do not adhere to your commands and you don't have the privilege to speak my family name."

Lancaster glared at him, but he didn't match him in size. As Gum continued to loom over him, Lancaster averted his gaze to...*me*. Me? Why me? But I felt the heat from his hatred burning through my chest. I squeaked as Caden brought me to him, a hand going to my hip, and pulling me behind him. As he did, Lancaster said, "My apologies, *Gum*."

Well. We could all tell how he thought of the replacement name. I could hear the sneer.

"Your problem is with these humans and this other worldly couple, but I warn you, Lancaster. If you make one move to harm any of these humans, you will face ramifications from me."

He returned to normal, and the building stopped shaking.

"These humans must not know of us. There are other

beings in the area. Families. Generations. We have lived here, feeling safe. If you allow these humans to know of us, that safety is gone. *Generations*."

"They won't tell–" She Shay started to talk.

"They will tell. It takes one word. One word. With the technology now available to them? They wouldn't even need to say it out loud, but they could do one video talking about the possibility of us existing. That would be enough. You know there are others out there looking for us, hunting us. They *cannot* find us. These humans would be hunted themselves."

Caden clasped me tighter to him.

"They'd be taken. Tortured. Wiping their memories isn't just for myself and my kind. It's for them as well. You have spent time with these humans. An evening now. Drank with them. Laughed with them. Talked with them. Do you want them to face those ramifications?"

Everyone got quiet. The weight of his words were felt. They were heavy. Oppressive.

But he was making sense.

I was not one to sign up for torture, and if this was the beginning of just one day knowing about them? I shivered at the thought of who these other beings are that would hunt them, would find us to find them.

I reached for Caden's hand gripping it hard.

He squeezed me, trying for reassurance.

"What about my brother and his girlfriend?"

She Shay glanced at Kellan before answering, "When I'll do the words, I'll include them in my mind. It'll happen simultaneously. It doesn't have to be in person for it to work."

Kennedy gave a small nod before sharing a look with her Shay.

He spoke, "It's okay." He took Kennedy's hand, stepping forward. "It's been a fun adventure, but if what you say is right, no one can hurt my family. I won't stand for it. If wiping my memory helps to save Kennedy, I'll do it." He said to Kellan, "We wouldn't give you permission before, but I do now."

Kennedy nodded, a tear sliding down her face. She looked my way and we shared a look.

We had such fun.

Mermaids.

The beach.

Finding out about demons and angels, and whatever Gum was.

We'd not know any of that anymore. We'd not know them anymore.

"...*These humans would be hunted themselves... Taken. Tortured...*"

Lancaster was right. It broke a piece of my soul to admit that, but he was. I stepped around Caden, raising my chin. "It's okay. This isn't our world. We don't know the rules, the consequences. If doing this helps to save you and us as well, we have to do it." I looked at Kellan, whose gaze was clouded and nearly all black. "I give you permission to remove any knowledge of yourselves and mermaids."

Caden sighed, pulling me to his chest and bending his head down. His lips grazed my forehead, but it was decided. We'd all do it.

If it was for the best.

GUM AND LANCASTER stood in the background as we were all lined up, side by side.

It was the same as how it happened the first time.

Kellan sent out some form of power, and Shay went to each of us, reciting the same words, adding in that we would forget spending time with them at the bar today. We would forget

Lancaster. We would only remember Gum as the friendly bartender.

I'd like to say that when it was done, I felt something missing, but that's not what happened.

On the last word she said, she repeated again from the beach, saying, "And now as your memories are taken, I fill in the gentle openings with laughter, love, and kindness. The magic will give us a pocket of time where we will leave, and once we are gone, everything will be complete."

As she finished, Kellan moved aside so he could see me.

Then, nothing.

I blinked, unsteady on my feet, and did I smell sulfur?

"Hey!" A bark came from the bartender. He was half glaring at us, and gestured to the clock. "We're past closing. You guys need to go."

"Why do I feel like I just passed out after a full day's bender, and I woke up on a bench in the park?" Kennedy came over, rubbing at her forehead.

I shook my head, a weird feeling settling through me. Like something was missing. "I don't know, but I have a headache, and I'm exhausted."

"Let's go, people! Let's go."

Caden headed over to pay our tab, but the guy didn't have to tell us again. I wanted to get out of there. Shay and Kennedy seemed of the same mindset.

12

———

We stayed for another three days, taking advantage of vacationing with our friends.

I loved it, but we never went back to that bar. Every time a local would recommend it, a sadness came over me. I couldn't explain it. I just knew I didn't want to go there, so we didn't. We went to all the other bars in the area. Restaurants. We went shopping. Walked on the beach. Spent time at Kennedy's brother's house.

When it was time to leave, we packed up our truck and didn't look at the code as we left the Airbnb we'd rented. It'd been such a steal to find at the last minute, but I knew we wouldn't be coming back so whatever the new code was wouldn't matter anymore.

As we drove to our next spot, we stopped in a gas station for a last fill-up.

I hopped out of the van, heading inside. "You want coffee?"

"No. Just water for me. Thanks, babe."

The door opened as I began to reach for it, and a guy came out. I started to go around him, a polite smile on my face, but he stopped midstep and stared at me.

I frowned, but then, there was something about him... Dark blond hair that was messy. It worked for him. Gave him a lazy aura, but no. I was wrong. A dangerous aura. He had sapphire eyes. And I was noting all of this in the back of my mind, as if I already knew him. That was silly. I'd never seen this guy before... No. Wait! I did. He and his girlfriend had come into the bar our first night here. Yeah, yeah. They sat and enjoyed the show in the background.

I gave him a smile, and a wave. "Hello. I hope you have a great day."

He blinked, before he nodded back. "You as well, Little Bee."

I had begun to move around him, but did a double take, my head snapping around to see him. He'd already started for his vehicle. I only saw his back. I watched him go to an expensive sports car and get inside. The girl in the front was stunning, and in a shocking and serene way. She said something to him as he got in, and if he replied, I couldn't tell, but then they left.

I got that same feeling I had when I thought of Mermaid Bar.

It was like an odd form of déjà vu, but not surreal. It was just an unwelcome feeling. I didn't like it, but I would forget it. I decided then and there.

Then my phone rang.

The kiddos were up from their naps.

13

———

Nine months later, I went into labor. It was in the middle of a contraction, as I was screaming at Caden because he'd done this to me, when I heard a voice in my head.

My head! What the hell?

"Summer."

"What?" I snapped at Caden.

He frowned. "What?"

"You said my name." I was panting. I had sweat covering every inch of my body, and I was not happy.

"No, I didn't."

"Summer, listen to me."

I looked around, because who the fuck was that? "Is someone's phone on?"

"You will remember, because right now you are with child. When you give birth, the pain will unsettle your mind. The coding we did to wipe your memories of us will be broken into pieces. I'm putting this into your memories so it will smooth everything for you. No ill effects will happen to you. You will be the only one to remember, and it's because you conceived your child here. Your child will bear a mark from this place. When you see it, you don't need to be afraid. This

place has magic in the air, and your child has that magic in her. Everywhere she goes, she will make people smile. They will feel her presence, and she will heal wounds inside of them without knowing it. She is special, and if she opens the door to this world someday, as her mother, you will be there to support her. Until then, until you bring her into this world, you will adhere to the coding Shay is putting into your mind."

I'd gone stark still, hearing that voice in my head, and in a flash, I saw him.

Kellan.

I saw her. Shay.

I saw–*ahhhhhh!* The mother fucking pain. Why hadn't I taken the epidural? Go natural my ass. Never fucking agai–*aahhhhhhhhhh!*

Four hours later, I was holding Circe Colton Banks.

When she opened her eyes, I remembered everything.

If you enjoyed, please leave a review!
They truly help so much.

Anti-Stepbrother
Hate To Love You
Evil

For more stories,
go to www.tijansbooks.com

ACKNOWLEDGMENTS

I wanted to write a little something for a Christmas surprise in my reader group, so I asked some of the girls who help out in there what they'd like. They suggested quite a few, but these were the three that stuck out to me. Anti-Stepbrother and Hate To Love You both were asking to update the readers, and Kellan never really stops glowering and making threats in my head, so there you go!

I hope you enjoyed!

This one was for the readers in my reader group. I really appreciate everyone in there.

And Bailey. I can't ever forget to thank my special pup. Ever. He reminds me daily to be thankful for him.

DAMIEN'S SISTER

AN EVIL HALLOWEEN SHORT
TIJAN

(Set before A Crossover Adventure)

CHAPTER 1

"You're Damien's sister, right?"

Since we were juniors, and since Damien was the 'big man' on campus, or one of them once he joined a fraternity, this was not a shock to me. Damien was also in the most popular fraternity on campus, or so he told me. I tended to believe him because this was a weekly occurrence.

Everyone knew Damien.

What was different about this question was because I wasn't being asked by a human.

She asked the question as we were leaving class, and I stopped in the hallway, giving her a once-over.

Yep. Not human.

Humans didn't give me the zing she was giving me, and I sensed into her, shifting around—*witch*. Then, just as quick, an image flashed in my head. Her, and her coven, doing some ritual. They were dancing around a fire, half-naked. Their arms and heads raised to the sky, and smack in the middle was my half-brother. I didn't normally have a problem with witches. If they noticed me, they avoided me. If Kellan was around me, they ran like a bat out of hell.

The problem I was having was that Damien had been pinned to a stake and he was bleeding right next to the fire.

You will leave my brother alone.

She sucked in a breath, her eyes bulging out from the invasion in her head. I could get in her head. She just couldn't get in mine. Because of that, she was scrambling backwards literally and metaphorically.

I didn't. I mean—he's cute. That's all.

I glared at her, starting to walk her back to a more private hallway. *Not the right answer. I saw what you and your coven are going to do to him.*

What?! I'm not in a coven.

Then there were more images. Her. Her laughing. Her friends. Them talking about college, about courses, about cute boys...about spells. Them practicing spells.

I got to the last image. A love spell.

Are you kidding me? You're going to bleed him so he falls in love with you?

Omg! No! I'd never do that to him—

I showed her the image I saw of her, him, the fire, the naked dancing.

Blood drained from her face. She was quaking at the sight of what I showed her.

A flicker of doubt sparked then.

I *was* seeing the future. Maybe something was wrong here?

We were now in a different hallway, one way more private. No one was coming past us. She stammered out, her gaze skirting around us, "I—I'd never do that to him. Not willingly, I mean. I have a crush on him. But that, what you're showing me —" She stopped, frowning at me. *What are you? I can't—I can usually feel a werewolf or a vampire.*

I snorted.

"I'm a little above your pay grade." *And so is my brother, by the way.*

I glared at her again.

I might not have met my half-brother under the best circumstances, but since then and since his family had taken me in, I was protective of him. I wanted to ground my teeth because me showing her that image should've changed the future's course.

It didn't.

It was still there. I saw it firmly rooted in her timeline.

I sighed. "It's Halloween. We're in college. You know there's an Alpha Mu party tonight because it's a fraternity. They're always going to throw a party. Now, because of you, I'm going to have to go." I shifted closer, making sure she heard me real clear. "And I'm going to be bringing my boyfriend."

Her eyes widened again.

I felt her air whoosh out of her. The hairs on the back of her neck stood up, and I felt that too. The air around us picked up in electricity, because if anyone was plugged into the supernatural scene, they knew who my boyfriend was.

And they avoided him.

"Kellan Braden," she whispered. "That's who I'm picking up on you." She was taking me in, all new now. The blood just kept draining from her. "He's all over you. He's—I thought it was a ridiculous rumor that he was here."

Going to school was putting it mildly.

His name was in the system.

He attended what classes he had with me. The registrar kept putting him in classes that weren't mine, because he declared a degree and they're trying to make sure he graduated on time. To them, he was a normal student. To Kellan, he could care less what classes he was in. It wasn't like he was going to use the degree. Damien and I, we were the gung-go college students. We were the ones who were hoping to get degrees and then careers.

Every class that I wasn't in with him, he used his power on

the professors and their TAs. He was given good scores across the board so he only showed up when I had class. Those classes, he sat with me, he listened with me, and he took the tests with me. He did the projects with me. If he was put in a different group, someone always magically insisted on switching with me so we were in the same group.

So, Kellan being a student here was a slight exaggeration.

But he was here, because of me.

And he was known to the supernatural world. To the non-supernatural world, girls only whispered about him because he still was hot, dangerous, and mysterious. But mostly, in that world, Damien was the big stud, and bless my brother's heart, but he cared about it. Kellan didn't.

Kellan cared about me.

And I loved him for it.

"You're going to tell me everything that your 'friends' might be planning. Got it?"

She moved her head in a quick nod. "Got it."

CHAPTER 2

The Alpha Mu's house was filled with humans.

Lots of humans.

College humans.

Drunk humans.

Scantily clad humans.

Kellan had been called for a meeting of the demon-variety, so the plan was that he'd meet me here as soon as it was done. Because of that, I walked inside by myself. I'd made a few friends from university, but since I knew we'd be attending a witches' brew later tonight, I didn't want to have anyone with me that I'd have to ditch later on.

It was the messenger side in me.

Booze, perfume, and sweat were the smells that hit me first once I was inside. I wasn't counting the rap because I'd heard it outside. The bass had been thumping.

At seeing me, two of the brothers dropped their jaws. "Hey —uh—you're Damien's sister."

There was that title again.

"Where is he?"

The one guy didn't like me being there, and he switched to glaring right away.

The other one gestured upstairs. "In his room."

I started for the stairs.

The scowling guy grabbed my arm—or he would've.

I turned, feeling the movement in the air and I shot into his head, *Do not touch me.* It was a warning only for him to hear. The other guy didn't know anything happened except that his friend started to reach for me, and didn't.

"Uh. He's got company, if you know what I mean." The nicer one's smile was a bit more tentative.

I separated from my body, moving upstairs and looking through the rooms.

The first room, a guy was playing video games.

Second room, a guy was eating licorice.

Third room, he was masturbating.

The next three rooms were couples having sex.

Room five and six were empty.

Damien's room was at the top, so I kept moving.

He felt me coming, sensing me.

I felt him meet me, speaking to me, *What are you doing here?*

I pushed forward, going into his room.

Stop!

Who are you with?

Someone. Stop it.

Is she the witch?

I felt his surprise before he growled in my head, *Stop, Shay. I'll come down in a second—*

I pushed the image of him bleeding into his head and then the rest of my encounter with the witch today.

They have a coven.

They're harmless.

I pushed that image again. *You're dead in this event.*

He was quiet, and I could hear him audibly sigh. *I'll be right down. I'm not with that girl.*

I began retreating, returning to my body, but there was a tingle on the back of my neck. I needed to see who the girl was.

Damien growled, feeling me still coming.

I said no!

I shoved through his wards, destroying them and I saw her. He was already rising, pulling his pants on. He halted, feeling me in the room.

Get out! Now!

I looked at the girl. She was panting, her face all red. Her hair was sweaty, and her lips were parted. She liked him, liked him a lot.

She was human. That was my first feeling.

I started to pull back, but that tingle started again.

I had to know...

I shoved into her head.

SHAY!

A roar in my head from him, and I could hear him. He was on his feet, sprinting down to me.

I was inside of her, going through her mind.

Her blood, though.

Her blood was calling to me.

I could taste it even though my body remained just inside the house.

He was thundering down the stairs, snarling as he pulled his arms through a shirt. "I said to get out of her head! That's a violation." He shoved past his two brothers, and at his words, those near us froze.

I was still in her head, or her blood to be more exact.

She's a born witch.

He growled in front of me, his hands curling into fists.

She doesn't practice.

Her ancestors are strong. Demonic.

Those are old old ancestors.

I pulled out of her now, coming back to my body and staring at him.

To the two gaping brothers, we were staring at each other.

We have a practicing coven on this campus, and you have a born witch in your bed. You do the math.

He growled again. *They'd have to have a superior skill set to do what you're insinuating. I'm a half-messenger. I wouldn't go down without a fight.* He softened. *And you're here now too. They'd be taking on two half-messengers.*

He wasn't adding the last bit. They'd be taking on a full-blooded demon as well.

"Hey! It's Damien's sister." An arm came down around my shoulders. I was jerked back to a sweating chest. A hand holding a beer was attached to that arm. "D, I forget every time how hot your sister is. Why don't you bring her around more? You partying with us tonight?"

One of the other guys let out a strangled laugh. "Uh, Pete, aren't you forgetting about—"

Damien's tone was frosty. "She has a boyfriend. Get your arm off of her, or he will rip it off. Trust me."

That was when I felt them.

They're coming, I said to Damien, already turning for the door.

They were out there, and they were spreading out.

Damien moved to stand next to me. *They're going to surround the house.*

I wasn't feeling a new coven. I was feeling power, old power.

I sighed. "They got someone with that skill set."

He cursed next to me.

They began moving forward.

"We have an entire house of humans."

The guy whose arm was around me tightened. "Humans? What the fuck you talking about, bro?"

I forgot him and shoved his arm off me by force.

I never touched him, but the air blasted him and he fell backwards a few steps before steadying himself. "Whoa. What was that, man?"

The chanting started after that.

CHAPTER 3

"Where's Kellan?" Damien yelled at me as we both charged out to meet them.

"He's at a meeting."

"A meeting? On Halloween?!"

"Oh cool! It's a show," someone said behind us.

A guy pushed past us, and a crowd had formed.

The witches weren't just college aged. There were older ones. A few ancients. Some boys and girls who could've been in high school. Most of them were harmless by themselves. Together, I felt their power zapping us.

Damien did too, cursing.

"Is that girl your girlfriend?"

He shot me a look, his eyebrows pulled together. "You want to have this talk now? We have to fight off a coven of witches, and somehow keep my cover intact."

"Kellan can wipe their minds."

"Kellan's not here!" he snapped at me, just as the witches began to raise their hands.

The chanting got louder with it.

"Cover." I pffted at that. "You talk like you're a cop or something."

"A what?!" From one of the fraternity brothers.

"He's not."

The guy didn't look like he believed me.

Damien cursed under his breath. "Where the hell is your boyfriend?"

More people came outside, spilling out so probably half the house was on the front lawn, and still drinking. A few of the girls were eyeing the witches, their noses wrinkled up.

"When did we book talent for the party?" Another of the fraternity brothers stepped out, coming over to Damien. "When have we ever booked talent for any party?"

Do not tell him the truth.

Damien shot me a look. *I'm fully aware. I'm not an idiot.*

You're sexing with a born witch. You do the math.

You're sexing with a full-blooded demon. You do the math.

Children, no fighting. Please. Kellan's soft chiding and amusement slid over our connection. No matter what Damien might say, he was relieved to have that full-blooded demon on our side, and here.

Where are you? I asked him.

Coming, and coming in fast. I have things to tell you.

Damien snorted. *Let me guess. Your meeting was to warn you about an uprising of witch activity in the area?*

Child. Patience. I know you're eager for me to save your ass, but I'm coming as fast as I can.

Damien flushed. "I hate it when he does that to me."

"Does what?"

"You know."

"What the fuck are you two talking about?"

"It's nothing."

"Dude." The guy scowled at Damien, jerking his thumb toward the witches. "And what the fuck is happening there? I'm starting to feel things, and I don't feel emotions unless I'm fucking. What the fuck's up with *that*?"

Damien muttered a curse. "We have to handle this."

"I'm here."

I heard Kellan the same moment I felt him. I felt him inside of me, a dark throbbing in my chest, and then our connection became crystal clear. That happened when we were in the same room. He materialized out of black vapor next to me, and someone screamed.

Thud.

The screamer fainted.

Someone saw you, Damien growled to Kellan.

Kellan shrugged before he grinned, moving closer to me. He dipped his head down, moving past me next. A slight graze of his lips on my shoulder. Tingles trailed from the touch, but then he was moving forward to the witches.

The fraternity guy scowled at Kellan, then the fainter. "I think I'm going to go back inside and pull out my CBD pen."

"You do that, Crowman." Damien nodded at him. "We'll handle crowd control out here."

"Yeah. You do that, bruh."

"Bruh."

More and more people were becoming aware of Kellan.

Authority rolled off of him in waves, along with a dark and deadly vibe. His presence was already affecting the witches. They felt his power, and with a flick of his hand, his power began permeating out of him in a more concentrated dose.

The chanting grew. Getting louder and louder. Their arms were at shoulder length, now moving upwards of the shoulder. Their palms were angled upwards to the sky.

The leader witch locked eyes with Kellan, frustration tightening her facial features. Her hair was blowing in the air. All their hair was blowing in the air. Each witch wore different clothing, but they were loose-fitting and they were billowing from the force of the wind.

Shay.

It was Kellan.

Yes?

I'll need your help for this.

I heard the whispering then.

He was commanding the humans to go back into the house.

One by one, they followed. Some were fighting the pull. Some went willingly, not knowing why they were going into the house. A few had blank expressions. A couple guys were frowning, their confusion emanating from them. They didn't know what was going on.

Go inside. Forget you saw this. Go inside. Forget you saw this.

It was Kellan sending out that command, over and over, in a low push to them all.

"Stop, Demon. We know who you are, and you do not deter us." The leader witch stepped forward, her hair now whipping furiously around her. Her chanting got even a louder, a deep baritone echoing around us. Her arms were almost all the way to the sky.

Damien stepped next to me. "Wonder what happens when they're fully pointing upright?"

It felt like a last click.

The pressure had been building, rising, and like the hour hand and minute hand on a clock became aligned, both pointing upwards too.

Whatever was going to happen, we were about to find out.

CHAPTER 4

Shay.

Kellan spoke in my head, but I didn't have time to react. His hand shot out to me, and I was pulled forward. I flew through the air, until his hand was on my stomach. It was hot, pressing in, but then I felt my power coming out of my body. He was using it, connecting to his, and then sending a black and white thread that looked like rapidly moving little particles. They were twisting around each other.

Both our powers were going to the witches, to each one individually.

He was knocking them out.

Kellan. What are you doing?

I'm removing each of their individual power source. They're trying to use the source of a witch inside the house. The one Damien was with.

You were eavesdropping too?

I'm connected to Shay.

That was Kellan's explanation, but contrary to what he was insinuating, we were not in each other's heads on a constant basis. So, he'd been eavesdropping.

I shot him a grin. Kellan saw and matched it, then he pulled more power from me. The white was starting to consume the black. It was becoming more and more bright, blinding to the witches.

The girl who had approached me on campus came from around the house, her hands back to being low and held out in front of her hips. Her hair was blowing in the wind, but it was also changing colors. Black. White. Silver. Red. Orange. Yellow. Blue. Green. Purple. It just kept changing, and then her voice grew.

I could see her own power. It was rippling up from the earth, moving into her and she was sending it out to her other coven members.

I was wrong.

She was their leader.

As if sensing my realization, her voice dropped even lower and it was booming now.

They're speaking their own language.

I growled. *Witch language.*

I hated witch language. It sounded like a mix of Russian and German.

"Damien?" a soft and tentative voice came from behind us.

We turned. It was Damien's girlfriend/maybe-just-a-hookup. Kellan and my power were circling around her, but there was an invisible string coming out from her stomach. I could see our power around the string, and it was pulling her toward the leader.

"What's happening to me, Damien?" Her voice hiccuped. She was visibly trembling.

"They're tapping into her blood, and using her ancestors' power."

I was glad Kellan knew, because I had no clue.

Neither did Damien, judging by his blank look that he sent me. "Can you stop it, Kellan?"

Before Kellan could reply, the leader girl spoke again, her voice even deeper. She had moved so she was directly in front of the house, and in front of us.

"You cannot. Our power is fierce. Our power is strong. Our power—"

"Your power is starting to give me a headache." Kellan moved toward Damien's girl, and he reached out for the invisible cord. His hand closed around it, and he looked back to the witch leader.

I knew my soulmate.

He'd been in a good mood until now. He'd been chilled and relaxed. This wasn't anything to get worked up over, but that was gone. The witches had fought enough where he was annoyed, and as I was seeing this, his face was darkening and the witches (those not unconscious) were clueing in too.

Their chanting started to break off. They started chattering, their voices raised in high pitches.

The leader ignored them, and she thrust her hands out, yanking on Damien's girl. "No! You will not—"

Kellan closed his hand over the string. With his eyes locked on the leader's, he taunted, "You're saying what now?" And just like that, he destroyed their connection to Damien's girl.

The image of my brother being tied to a pole around their fire vanished. I was watching, and it was instead being replaced with Damien's fraternity house being on fire.

"She's going to burn the house down!" I cried out because that *was* something to worry about. We got all the humans inside.

Damien cursed, now comforting his girl-whatever-she-was.

"You!" A feral scream came from the leader to Kellan. She was enraged, actual fire in her eyes. "You will not stop us. You cannot stop us. We were many. We are eternal. We will never stop—"

Kellan rolled his eyes and raised his hand in the air. In one snap, he released my power and sent his to surround each witch. It happened in two seconds.

His power completely overtook them, and then he snapped his fingers.

The witches were gone. Poof. Just like that.

I reeled around to him. "You killed them."

He sighed. Some particles left over flew past on the wind, and he raised his finger, sending the wind away from us. Then he rubbed his hands clean. "Well. Yeah. I'm a demon." He smirked. "This is my Christmas Day. Happy Halloween to me. I got to kill some witches." He came over, leaning in to kiss me.

I was too shocked to do anything.

I wanted them stopped, not killed.

He said against my lips, grazing me, "They didn't have souls, Shay." His hand came up and wrapped around the back of my neck. His thumb spread up, further holding me steady. "No matter what side you're on, a human without a soul is dangerous. These were witches without them. They'd already sold them to a different demon for their power source. They were weakening, that's why they had to use the born witch. They were going to try to use hers to tap Damien for the rest of his messenger power. I *had* to kill them."

"Oh."

I relaxed, letting the usual love and warmth take over me whenever Kellan was near. He pressed his lips back to mine, and desire raced through me. I surged up, my arms wrapping around him as I opened my mouth for him and his tongue slipped inside.

Damien coughed, clearing his throat. "Seriously? Right here? I was hoping to introduce you to Sacha."

Kellan ignored him, tilting his head for better access.

My hands were splayed out, pressing into his neck.

I couldn't get enough of him.

"Um." A timid cough from her. "Hi. I'm Sacha."

"She's my girlfriend." Damien's voice was flat.

Then the door burst open.

The music from inside grew louder, clearer, and a distinctive aroma sailed outside to us. All the while, Kellan and I kept kissing.

We'd come a long way.

Kellan enjoyed killing, but he didn't like murdering. There was a distinction to him, and he just killed thirty witches. Or I was guessing on the number. I didn't take the time to count them, but his hands were growing more demanding and I knew it was a matter of time before we needed to be alone.

Kellan pressed against me.

He was showing no indication of stopping.

I moved my face so I could see Damien.

He was watching us with his eyes bugged out, glaring. "Really? Now?"

I sighed, feeling Kellan wrap his arms around me. He was getting ready to portal us away.

There's a human here. From Damien.

Your girlfriend doesn't count. From Kellan as his tongue was sliding against mine. He was making my insides ache and throb.

I'm not talking about her. Crowman is right here.

Who's Crowman?

If you'd stop trying to eat my sister's face, you'd see my fraternity broth—

I closed my eyes, stilling in Kellan's arms. He shouldn't have said a word because as soon as he did, Kellan lifted his head. He looked at Crowman, who was swaying and holding a beer in his hand. His eyes were wild and dilated. He was sweating and had pit stains under his arms leading halfway down his shirt.

He's drunk.

So?

Kellan rolled his eyes, then tightened his hold.

We were going anyways.

I smiled at the girl. "It's nice to meet you. Is that your friend coming out?"

She turned to look.

Kellan portaled us out of there, and as we went, we heard: "Who?"

And from Crowman, "Dude. You're human, right?"

Then we were back in our room, on our bed, and Kellan was on top of me, pressing into me.

I rested my head back on the pillow, smiling at him as he rose over me. His eyes were dark and hungry.

"Happy Halloween."

His eyes smoldered, and he leaned down to me again. "Happy Halloween right back at you."

He began to move down my throat, lingering just above my chest.

That's when I remembered his meeting.

"Wait. What happened at your meeting?"

He took my hands and pinned them beside my head. "I got the orders to take down a soulless witch coven. They reneged on a deal with their demon so they were going anyways. I was just able to have more fun this way. Now." He pressed firmly against me and moved up, grinding on me. "Are we celebrating Halloween naked this year? Or in costumes?"

I hope you enjoyed this very short bonus scene from Evil!
Stay tuned for A Kellan Christmas.

A KELLAN CHRISTMAS
AN EVIL CHRISTMAS SHORT

(Set after Damien's Sister)

TIJAN

Humans are so simple with their holiday traditions.
They are ignorant of the powerful and majestic creatures
among them, like me.
I am the most powerful demon above the surface.
Nothing can stop me...except, well, some stupid prophecy.

CHAPTER 1
KELLAN

I don't do celebrations unless they're the worshiping-your-demon sort of thing. I'm all for those, because *duh*—they're worshiping me.

Not Shay. Oh no. She likes parties and holidays and events where people dress up, smile, and laugh.

I also laugh on these occasions. I laugh *at* them, but she says they're laughing *with* each other.

Right.

Anyway, I'm down for Halloween. That's like a shrine made into a whole night of worshiping me. Humans have no idea the root of some of their "customs."

But Christmas...

My girlfriend, a lovely messenger. (That's the term we use for those celestial beings up above. I refuse to use the A-word unless we're calling them assholes, which I'm game for.) But back to my girlfriend, who is not an asshole. Shay *loves* Christmas.

She gets all glassy-eyed when it comes to Christmas.

That's the day all demons go into hiding. Who wants to be around to celebrate that kid's birthday? But I love Shay. She's the whole reason I came topside and all that jazz. So yeah, if my girl wants to celebrate the prick's birthday, I guess I'll have to participate.

But a part of me is hoping to see some form of action. For Halloween, there was a thing with a coven of witches, so who knows. Maybe one came back as a demon, and even better, they want vengeance on me.

Now that'd be a great Christmas.

"Kellan."

This holiday was off to a bad start already. I turned, seeing Shay's half-brother coming toward me. Shay was in class, and I was waiting for her. Now I was questioning my demon sanity. Could I go soft? Would that make me go dumb too? I mean, waiting for her in this hallway—where her building attached to the main college campus center—was stupid of me.

Although, I did note the way the college students were moving past me, giving me a wide berth. Good humans. They *could* be trained.

"You waiting for Shay?" Damien asked, stopping to talk to me like we were friends.

He even looked like he believed this—not fazed, not in fear of me. He watched the humans, but not the way he should have. He was half-messenger, or a little less than half of a messenger. Yes, they're all saintly and annoying—or at least he was—but he had *power*. These humans were nothing. They were ants for us to step on. Why didn't he get that? Why didn't other messengers?

I'd met a few full-blooded messengers. They weren't as saintly as Shay and her brother. I was convinced something had gone wrong in their birth. The full-blooded messengers were dicks.

"What's up?" I asked, before seeing who else was with him.

God.

I mean, not Him. *Shit.*

Devil.

No. That didn't have the same effect.

I'll stick with what I know—*hell.*

Damien wasn't alone. I hadn't noticed them. Why would I? They were ants, as I mentioned. But these were Damien's fraternity brothers. He cared about them the way a human would care for a pet.

"What's up with you?" Damien frowned at me.

I frowned back. Oh—I'd already been frowning. So, I glared.

Shay liked to call me on my look of death. I guess I was letting it fly now, but good for me.

Shay didn't think I missed killing humans.

I did.

A dark, sensual pleasure came from crushing one of those ants. And the more, the merrier. It'd been too long since I'd wreaked havoc.

I eyed Damien's frat brothers. They seemed like idiots who could be easily pulled a certain way. Maybe I could get them to sell their souls to a demon, have them go back on their deal, and I could be sent after them? Or hell, I'd just go after them. I'd turn vigilante for my kind, no problem.

No demon would care.

"Shay's coming."

Right. *Fuck.*

I slammed my shields in place. I'd kept them down, but I needed to fortify them now. Shay had been distracted. She'd been in class, but now all she'd need to do was walk toward me, and she'd be able to tell something was up.

I kept her out when I was feeling extra murder-y. That vibe tended to upset her, and who could blame her? That was the messenger side of her. Also, that was just Shay. I loved her. I couldn't pick her apart. She accepted me, so I wasn't a hypocrite. That's something non-demons were, but not us. We demons were upfront and honest about our dark side.

"What's going on?"

I bit down a curse because that was her—her voice in my head—and I could feel her concern. She'd connected to me, so she knew something was up.

I added a second and third layer of walls, keeping her out.

I could sense her internal gasp. *"Why are you doing that? What's going on?"*

"It's finals, sis." Damien had picked up on our dialogue. *"Brings out the evil side of all of us."*

Shay rounded the bend in the hallway, coming from her building to where we were standing. Damien and I both watched, waiting.

His friends looked between us, then down to where we were watching.

One's eyebrows furrowed together. He'd been drunk the night of Halloween, but me appearing from the black mist in front of him must've stuck. He knew something was off, but he didn't ask any questions today. Instead, he just paid attention. The other friends were ranking girls as they walked by.

"That's a five, but man—those tits. Good handful. I could make them bounce. They could jiggle so good—"

I tuned out his thoughts, and Shay turned the corner.

I felt knocked back on my heels. It happened whenever we were in the same room. Our connection sizzled, strengthening as she approached, and I felt her nudging at my walls. *"What's in there, Kellan? Why am I concerned?"*

I gently moved her back. *"Just the holidays. I'm okay."*

She frowned, still coming toward us. Other students were walking around her, passing in front of her, but I only had eyes for her. She was the boat in the waves. She came to a stop in front of me, ignoring her brother's presence as she looked into my eyes.

She lifted a hand, caressing the side of my face with her fingers.

Her touch was soft, loving.

"What's in there? Why are you keeping me out?"

I shook my thoughts clear, feeling the last of the rage slipping away, and I lowered the shields. As I did, she came in, looking around. I reached for her, my hand going to her waist, and drew her to me. I leaned in to touch her forehead softly with mine, but she didn't seem to notice. She was still looking in my head, reading my thoughts, feeling my emotions.

Finding nothing—or nothing I hadn't wanted her to know—she pulled back a little, still frowning. She tipped her head back and dropped her voice. "I don't like secrets."

I shook my head. "No secrets. Not from you."

"That's a lie—"

My mouth was on hers, and as I knew it would, the kiss pushed her little resistance aside, distracting her completely.

I was a demon. We're all assholes.

CHAPTER 2
STILL KELLAN

"Kellan, dude."

My blood froze. The human was *not* talking to me.

I looked.

His mouth moved, grinning as he stuffed a rolled-up piece of pizza inside. "What are you and the missus doing for Christmas?"

It was.

He was talking to me.

Damien's pet gestured toward Damien, who had frozen beside him. "This one just says you all are going home for the break but won't say when."

I narrowed my eyes.

Did this child not have any sense of self-preservation? Did he not realize what could happen if I was in a bad mood?

Damien shot me a look.

I'm sure Shay would be miffed if I turned this human into mist, but I entertained the thought. This was the human who seemed to be getting an indication there was something not of human descent about the three of us.

Crowman, they called him.

Crowman was stupid.

I leaned forward and held up my hand. "I could break your neck with the snap of my fingers."

He stopped chewing. His eyes lifted to study me.

Study. Pfft.

He should fear me.

I *was* going soft. I'd been around too many humans, been in love—no, not that. This wasn't Shay. I loved her with everything in me, the good and bad, but I was a *demon*. I'd been ignoring my roots for too long.

A bit of the rage from before began swirling inside of me.

It crept in through cracks I'd ignored, and it began filling me.

Shay gasped in my head.

Shit.

She was in here. I tried to push her out, but—

"*No, you won't!*"

Damien's eyes went wide. "*What's wrong? What's going on?*"

The darkness had nearly engulfed me. At Shay's discovery, it pushed faster, coming with more ferocity.

I *did* want to kill this human.

Kill him. Kill him.

I did. I actually wanted to do this.

There was a faint sound of chairs scraping in the background, but I was focused on him. He froze completely. I had a hold on him. He couldn't move, not an inch. His eyes rolled in their sockets. I could smell the frantic fear on him, and if I were letting him move, he would've run by now.

I sensed others leaving the dining hall. The room was fast emptying.

Other humans had better life instincts than this one.

"Kellan!" Shay's nails sunk into my arm, and she wrenched it from the table. "No!"

She yanked me out of whatever spell I'd been in.

I looked around and realized the black mist wasn't just *in* me. It was all over the room, filling it up, going into every corner.

I turned, almost dazed, and realized I was still holding Damien's friend. I had paralyzed him. I released him, and he scrambled backward. His pants were wet. He hit the floor on his back but was immediately back up and took off for the exit.

"What just happened?" Damien stood, stepping back from the table. He moved to stand between his friend, who was out of the room by now, and me.

Shay groaned and snapped her fingers.

The smell of smoke mixed with my mist.

A moment later, someone yelled, "Fire!"

The alarm sounded.

It was only the three of us left, and for a beat, no one said a word.

I fought the rage, trying to suck the mist back inside me. But it lingered in the air.

"Wha—" Damien started to speak when the door opened behind him.

The alarm grew louder, and his friend—the one I had frozen—stepped back in the room. His face was set, guarded, his fists opening and closing at his side. Then, he lifted his head, his hands unfisted, and he strode back toward us.

Shay moved to stand between him and me.

I moved to the side so he could still see me, and his gaze never wavered.

A few yards away, he stopped and looked at Damien for a second. Then back to me.

"What just happened?" he asked.

I snorted, but Shay rounded on me, giving me her look of death.

I shut up.

"Crow—" Damien stepped toward him.

"No, dude." He moved back a step, and Damien halted. He looked back at me. "I know something just happened, and I know you did it. I—" His throat moved up and down. He blinked a few times, rapidly, before his chest lifted and held. "I couldn't move, and I knew you were going to kill me. I..." He edged back another step. "To tell the truth, I still feel like you're going to kill me."

He was right. I still wanted to.

The black mist thickened and swirled around in the room.

Crowman saw it and moved to the side.

"That's smoke," Shay said.

He turned to her and looked up.

The mist had engulfed the room's sprinkler. Yet not one drop of water had come out of it.

"That's not smoke."

"*Kellan.*" A loud voice filled the space.

Shay sucked in her breath. Damien did too before both sets of eyes went to me.

"Who is that?" Damien asked.

I ignored him.

"*What?*" I asked impatiently

"*You need to come to me, son.*"

Like hell I would. "*How are you reaching me?*"

"*I can always reach you. You need to come to me. I need to speak to you.*"

"No—"

"*It's about your messenger—*"

No! "NO!" Shay screamed that in my head and out loud, but I was gone.

Anything that had to do with her, I would always put her first—even if it *was* Satan himself calling to me.

CHAPTER 3

KELLAN IN HELL NOW

It takes a while to get to hell, which I guess is kinda fitting, given the theme of it being hell. It's not a short trip down or up. I knew my father could've been toying with me, baiting me by saying this was about Shay, but he'd never done that before.

If it was a lie, he was planning something else. What that was, who knew? But there would've been rumors. Other demons would've been skittish when they saw me. I would've felt the Earth rumbling—that actually happened sometimes. I would've smelled the deceit.

For us higher demons, that was a thing. Fear. Lies. Sexual arousal. Everything had a smell. Everything had its own energy. We could tap into all of it.

And truth also had its own feel, texture, smell.

I'd smelled truth from my father. Hence me coming down here.

Shay was pissed. I could feel it from her. We were still connected. We'd always be connected, but I'd put so many guards and walls around her now. I didn't want her feeling and sensing everything alongside me once I did get through the barrier. And what would be worse was other demons picking up that I was bonded to a half-messenger.

I was sure they could feel her presence on me, so the more distance in our connection, the better.

Demons loved torturing messengers. Some would gladly die for one chance to unleash pain on a messenger. They didn't care what kind of messenger—half, full, an asshole, or someone loved like Shay. They didn't care. The hate went deep.

When I arrived at the barrier, I could feel the guards on the other side.

They never stopped anyone from coming down here. All were welcome. But once you got in, staying in one piece was another story.

I moved through the barrier, and immediately the guards corporealized and moved toward me.

I knew them. Both were higher demons, guards for my father.

"You knew I was coming," I said.

Aardvin moved forward, his eyes gleaming.

Why wasn't I surprised he'd picked a hideous body? There were boils on his skin, warts, and sores festering. He'd always been *off* in his tastes about who to torture.

"We're here to escort you to your father," he said. "He wants to make sure you arrive...alive. You've been above for so long, we thought you might've gone *soft*." He hissed the last word, finding enjoyment in the insult.

This whole show was an insult, this thinking I wouldn't be able to travel through the Underworld to my father.

I was already moving.

A scythe appeared before me, and I grabbed it, acting before either of them could react.

A slice to the left, a step forward, and another slice to the right. Since they had corporealized, their heads slid off, falling with a thud to the ground.

Their eyes rolled toward me, their mouths still in smirks.

They weren't dead. The rules were different in the Underworld, but it'd be a bitch for them to reattach when I was done, and they needed to reattach before moving back to their noncorporeal forms.

I raised the scythe and went to work. "You got it all wrong," I told them. "I've been resting. Now I'm all charged up."

I didn't leave them in pieces when I'd finished.

They were in slivers.

CHAPTER 4

BLOODY KELLAN

They weren't the last.

More demons met me on the path.

The scythe appeared each time.

It wasn't mine. The scythe appeared for me. If I weren't supposed to, it wouldn't have shown itself. When they appeared, it was considered an honor in the Underworld.

As a result, when I got to my father's residence, I was covered in blood. It dripped down my arms and fingers. My legs were soaked in it. I left bloody footprints behind me, all the blood of others.

It was glorious, and the demon in me writhed in pleasure.

On his front steps was a large podium, a hundred stairs leading up into the sky, up to where he looked down upon me.

That's when I knew he loved this.

He loved what I had done.

I had fed my demon, and he knew it.

His nostrils flared, smelling the blood on me. I could sense his pride. *"You are still my son."*

His words drifted down to me, on a breeze he had created for them.

I didn't respond because I couldn't deny it.

I was who he had borne.

No other guards came out to meet me. They were there, but they were hiding or holding back on my father's orders. Either way, I ignored them and turned into my non-corporeal self. I moved up, floating to the podium my father stood on.

He didn't non-corporealize. He waited, studying me, sensing into me. He was probably picking up things I didn't want him to know, things I didn't know myself, so I tried to resist him. He was my Master, and I was his son, so a thread of resistance was built into me when I was born. It was the natural order for a son to defy his father.

I had been using that muscle the entire time I was gone, building it up, making it stronger. It was now my spinal cord, and it throbbed under my father's perusal.

He took the form of an old man, his skin wrinkled, his hair white. He had a slight hunch to his back, but it was all a guise. He could take any form he wanted—human, animal, alien. He could even show his wings, though I'd only glimpsed them once in my life.

"I'm here," I told him. *"Tell me why I'm here."*

He hissed, glaring, the wrinkles moving around his mouth. *"Respect, my son. It still works that way down here."*

Maybe.

My spinal cord retracted, growing veins and roots, grabbing hold of my other nerves and bones with a firm grip. I was still non-corporeal, but I could feel my resistance shifting, adapting. It was molding, making almost a new skin. I wondered what I would look like when I retook my human body.

But I was more powerful in this form. *"I am here. That is a form of respect. You know I've defied you, remaining above and with Shay."*

He hissed at her name, coiling backward. *"You will not use

her name. I can smell her on you. It's disgusting." His eyes flashed, smoke coming from them.

"She is my soulmate. You will show respect for that. I am bonded with her."

"I'm aware. I can feel her presence even now. She's more powerful than you think. She can see things you don't want her to see, read your thoughts. She's in your mind when you don't know she is. She is a plague. I never should've let you go above to get her for me."

For him.

I defied him there first, staying and not returning with her. But he wasn't entirely displeased.

"What is it that you have to share with me?" I asked.

This was not the most respectful conversation with the King of the Underworld, but he would not have called for me if he didn't want to have it. I would not have been allowed entry as easily as I was. Entire armies could have stood between myself and him, but none of that had happened.

In his way, he had given me a path of gifts. I had murdered them, but that was the gift. That told me everything.

He wanted me to hear whatever he had to say.

I just needed to wait him out. That, and try not to get killed.

He was silent a long time. I remained quiet, also showing respect in this way.

"There is a prophecy," he finally said.

There it was. I knew it.

I *hated* prophecies.

CHAPTER 5
FUCKING PROPHECIES

I could feel Shay calling to me, pulling at me to return to her.

I was moving, still traveling in my non-corporeal self, but I kept her locked out of my mind. I needed space to think about what my father had told me.

"A fallen messenger is coming. His wings were taken, and he will amass a great battle to win his way back to the heavens. He will find his answer in your soulmate. She is bonded to you and, therefore, seen as a plight to the Messenger ancestry. He will seek to eradicate her and further take out the good in you. He will then battle you, sending you back to the Underworld, ridding Earth of both ends of the soul-bond. When this happens, his wings will be returned to him, and he will be allowed entry back to the beyond. This is how it is said."

When the words left my father, I knew they were true. I felt the power of the prophecy, felt the roots they stemmed from, and it was not from him. He had not created the prophecy.

If Shay were killed, he was right—she was the only good in me. I would be a full-blooded demon if I weren't bonded to her.

"Kellan."

I felt her now, heard her voice in my head, and I allowed her in.

"What's going on?"

She felt my concern, and now I could feel hers.

"I'm coming back to you."

"What did your father say?"

I let her go through my thoughts.

When she was done, I felt her withdrawal before she asked, *"You think he's telling the truth?"*

I moved to her, prodding into her mind. I wanted access to what she was thinking. I could feel her fear and also her surprise that my father would be truthful.

"You think he's telling you this because he's your father?"

"I don't know."

"I can sense your worry, but we've battled other messengers before."

I didn't respond because this would be different. The prophecy had already been spoken. It would happen. This messenger was unlike the others. He had a mission, a quest. He would be committed. He would be brimming with power.

I could already feel the battle coming.

I would have to prepare Shay, but that wasn't for now.

I needed a distraction. *"Tell me about the holiday plans you have. I know you've been conspiring against me while I was gone."*

I sensed her smile as she relaxed, just a little. *"I have!"*

She told me while I traveled back to her.

Damien's fraternity was having a party. Some of Shay's college friends wanted to do a Christmas cocktail event on a rooftop of a building. It was going to be classy, so we needed to dress up. There would be caroling. And a hayride with eggnog.

And the worst one—

"I want to put a Christmas tree up in our house."

CHAPTER 6
SHAY'S TURN

Kellan was scared.

That said everything.

I knew he was shielding parts of the prophecy. I could feel his walls, and I probed, but he didn't want me to hear it all. I didn't understand why, but I had to trust him. He was my soulmate. He wouldn't keep it from me unless I wasn't supposed to know. But I knew he was scared.

And now I was, too. Immediately, I felt his regret.

That's why he didn't want me to hear it all. He didn't want this result.

I made a concerted effort to shove out my fear.

I replaced that with trust, love, and assurance.

Kellan could feel me doing this, and he knew why. It was my way of letting him know it was okay, the way he wanted to fight this prophecy. I would let him take the lead.

"I love you."

He landed, and I heard him out loud, then felt him.

I whipped around, and there he was, turning into his corporeal self in the kitchen, right behind me.

I stood up from the couch, where I'd been sitting, and got only two feet toward him.

He finished finalizing his transition, and then he caught me. I was in the air, in his arms, and his mouth was on mine.

"*Home. You're mine,*" he said.

I sighed. "*You're mine.*"

We went upstairs.

His mouth was commanding. His tongue moved in.

Lust and pleasure wound through me, zinging me.

My body heated. I needed him.

The time he took to go to his father and back hadn't been that long—a few days, but it felt longer. Like months. Space and distance in any form weren't supposed to come between bonded souls, but it'd been necessary.

I'd ached for him while he was gone, but now he was here, and that ache was throbbing.

I wanted more. Of him.

He laid me down on the bed and began tasting me.

The corner of my lips.

The side of my face.

My throat.

My chest.

Between my breasts.

My right breast. My nipple.

My left. The left nipple.

He kept moving down. His tongue moved over me, sensually caressing.

I could barely endure it.

I felt myself coming apart at the seams, wanting him, but he held off. He bent over me, moving farther down.

Down.

My stomach.

His hands went to my pants, hooked into the waistband, and pulled them down.

Rising, his mouth moved as his hands skimmed over my hips, taking hold of my panties.

He slid two fingers underneath each side. A trail of goose bumps and shivers followed, igniting the ache inside of me.

I could feel the throb. It had its own heartbeat.

He looked up, his eyes finding mine, his mouth lowering as he pulled my panties down my legs. Then I felt his lips on my clit, his tongue moving, tasting me.

A shattering sensation of pleasure ripped through me, and I gasped, my back lifting off the mattress.

He placed a hand on my stomach, holding me down, and he continued.

His tongue moved in.

Out.

Tasting me.

Filling me back up.

He gave a hard thrust, then a gentle rub right after. He kept thrusting, and he held me down all the while.

"Kellan!" I cried aloud.

"Not yet."

"Now!"

"Not yet."

I could hear his amusement.

I tried to bring my legs around him, squeezing him in protest, but he used his senses to hold me in place.

"What are you doing?"

He didn't answer, his powers now holding me fully immobile. I was pinned in place as he kept tasting me.

Another thrust.

The pleasure built.

Out.

The ache tripled.

In.

Quadrupled.

Out.

Five times strong.

I pleaded with him. "*Please, Kellan.*"

"*Not. Yet.*"

He moved over me but didn't enter. Instead, he slid his tongue farther inside, but then I felt him breach my body. He was merging with me completely—soul to soul.

I cried out. We'd done this before, but there was an extra emotional element here.

He was half corporeal. The other part was inside of me, caressing me everywhere.

My body shook.

I needed release.

He paused.

I wept, a tear sliding down my cheek. Everything was too much—yet amazing. I couldn't handle it.

I felt his soul as it grazed against mine.

And I burst.

The climax roared through me, and I could hear myself screaming—out loud, in his mind, and in mine. Then, before I finished coming, my body still trembling and shaking, he entered me fully.

His mouth came to mine, and he started all over again, bringing us both to another release. But for me, it took a *looong* time.

CHAPTER 7

A REPLETE KELLAN

I fortified our bond.

Shay didn't seem to notice during our lovemaking, but I did this throughout the entire night. Time after time, I reached for her, and each time, my soul cemented our bond.

Bonds are supposed to be permanent anyway, but with this prophecy…I was worried. I'm sure my father hadn't told me all of it, the demon side of him acting on it and holding some back. That's the part I couldn't prepare for.

So, this was my fail-safe.

If the prophecy came to fruition—and prophecies did tend to happen—Shay would be killed. Not her soul, though. I wouldn't let that happen. As I kissed her, caressed her, I wove our binds together so that if her body were destroyed, her soul would come to me.

In a way, I would own it, but only until she would get another body.

I couldn't lose Shay.

I could not.

I would not.

This was how it had to be.

It was early in the morning now, and I looked over.

Her body was exhausted. Her soul was more than content. But still, I felt the edge moving in me at the thought of losing her.

I reached for her again.

I moved her on top of me, facing away, and then I slid inside.

She gasped, her body bending backward, her breasts arching into the air.

I reached out, holding onto one, my other hand at her hip as I guided and moved with her, and I kept weaving.

CHAPTER 8
FRATERNITY KELLAN

Shay had said we'd go to a Christmas party put on by her brother's fraternity, so here we were on the Alpha Mu's front step. The house was decked out in fake snow, candy canes lined their sidewalk, a giant inflatable snowman wearing a bikini top but no bottoms and holding a joint sat next to the house, and they had phony reindeer set up in the front yard.

"Bah-humbug, my homies."

The brother who opened the door in the world's ugliest holiday sweater gave us the greeting, and I instantly wanted to smite him. Just because.

He took a look at Shay and frowned. "Not cool. Chicks are supposed to be decked out in slutty Christmas angel costumes."

He did *not* say that, not in front of me.

Shay glanced my way, feeling my wrath, but the dude was impervious. He looked my way, saw that I wasn't abiding by the ugly sweater rule either, and his frown deepened. Then he finally saw my face.

His frown disappeared. He swallowed and took a step back. "I mean, welcome to the festivities." He cleared his throat. "Uh, may your night be filled with debauchery, your drinks plentiful, and may you find your way home in the literal or *scoring* way." He winked, but his throat was still trembling when he was done.

"Down, Kellan."

Damien swept into the room, appearing from I had no clue where, and I didn't care because my demon had not been satisfied. I wanted to demolish this human in the most glorious and bloody way. I wanted to feel his blood dripping from my hands—

"Okay."

Shay's voice in my head stopped my thoughts cold.

"Calm down," she added, touching my bicep.

Damien stood between his fraternity brother and me. He didn't say a word.

I was on the edge, teetering there.

If I fell, I'd take everyone with me I could—all souls.

I'd never been this much on edge, ever.

"Something is wrong with me."

Damien grunted. *"You think?"*

"He has this new bloodthirst. I noticed it before his dad summoned him—"

"HIS DAD SUMMONED HIM?"

I shared a look with Shay. Had we not shared that with him? I guessed from his bulging eyes that we had not.

Both Damien and Shay were in my head, but I shoved them out. *"I need space."*

I felt Shay's hurt gasp. This was becoming a pattern, but I couldn't do anything about it.

I wanted to hurt.

I wanted to maim.

I wanted to destroy.

I wanted to bring the Underworld here, and I wanted to start with this fucking fraternity party.

I tore through the house, going straight for the liquor. The ants moved aside for me, like the parting of the sea. The females liked to look at me. It was always like that—in high school, at college. Some were braver than others, trying to approach me. The males usually had better instincts, staying *way* the fuck away from me. But they *all* scattered for me today.

Alcohol did nothing to me, not usually. A demon could get drunk or high from a kill or sex, but that was mostly it. Still, I was going to try.

Shay had been right. My bloodthirst was greater, but it wasn't sudden. It'd been rising in me for a while. There'd been a jolt, electrifying it.

It had grown and grown, and now, it was almost out of control.

I can't trust myself around Shay.

No. That wasn't right.

Shay was the *only* one I could trust myself around.

I frowned, pulling back that thought. I brought it front and center, examining it.

That wasn't *my* thought.

The realization stunned me.

Someone else was in my head, but they were making my thoughts sound and feel as if they were mine.

"Who are you?" I roared into the cavern of my mind.

A giggle. That was the response.

It sounded like a child's laugh, a sick and evil child—like a six-year-old torturing an animal and loving it.

"Get out. Now," I commanded, and I felt the voice leave my head.

"Show yourself," I spoke aloud in Angelic tongue. All beings had to follow a summons from that language, but so few knew how to speak it.

"You know my language."

I scowled, stepping back and bringing up my offenses. This was the Messenger.

"You're here for the prophecy." I sneered. "I can feel the shame emanating from you. It's loathsome."

He was near the back, in the shadows. He hadn't fully corporealized himself.

He was quiet.

I could feel him studying me.

I frowned. Something was wrong.

"How long have you been in my head?"

He jerked, his misty form spreading out before coming back together and firming. Finally, he spoke in hisses, "I've been with you since the beginning of time."

The fuck? "What?"

"I can see your father's been spreading tales. You should know better than to believe him."

"I sensed his honesty."

"I've always been with you, Kellan. I am you. I was with you when you went to him, but he drew you across the boundary. He knew I would separate, could separate from you."

"The prophecy was about a fallen Messenger. The last messenger I battled put up more of a show, to be honest."

"I am no messenger," he hissed. "I am you. I am your darkness."

"I'm a full demon. The only good in me is Shay's bond."

"That's not true. You have layers of us, and you have neglected us over the years. You have remained topside, falling in love with a half-messenger. Your demon is coming apart."

"You said you were able to separate when I went across the boundary?"

"Each time you do, more of us are able to separate from you."

I wasn't going to waste my time wondering what truth my

father *had* been speaking. I shouldn't have been surprised he used deception. That was his job.

"Why would my father want you to separate from me?"

"Because he can call upon us. We are still leashed to you. We are a part of you, but he can call on *us* to do his bidding."

Well.

Shit.

"I've been called to destroy your half-messenger," he announced. "The prophecy wasn't that a fallen messenger would destroy her. It was that *you* would destroy her. I'm here to fulfill the prophecy."

CHAPTER 9

SHAY

Crowman was showing me the fraternity's collection of Christmas trees. The first tree had been a gigantic inflatable tree. The second was an inflatable snowman. It had scarves wrapped around it, a star on the top, and beer kegs at the bottom to act as a base.

The third was smaller, made of rolled-up magazines. Different colored beer bottles had been placed on top, and I was told not to touch the magazines.

Tree number four was perched in the kitchen and made out of beer cans, with a smattering of red Solo cups as decorations. There was also a bra hanging from the top, instead of a star or an angel.

"Doesn't it look pretty?" Crowman nodded to himself, a beer in one hand and the other rubbing over his stomach.

His eyes widened as a scream came from the other room.

I knew that was bad, and the hairs on the back of my neck stood up, so I doubly knew it was bad.

I was turning away from Crowman, already reaching out to Kellan in my head, when I saw the demon.

Or—I thought it was a demon.

It was black mist, not fully formed to make a person, but definitely evil, and it was moving through the house as if it were in a race. It floated down the stairs, around the living room, and more screams rang out.

I was having déjà vu.

There were shouts, some laughs.

"Oh, cool!" someone yelled. "How are they doing that?"

"Wrong holiday, dudes. It's not Halloween," someone else chimed in. "Yo! Whatever you are."

The black mist stopped in midair, and the top half tilted to the side as if, as if pausing to listen.

The guy raised his beer in the air. "Turn into a Christmas elf!"

"Or Santa!"

"Rudolph."

The black mist didn't do anything for a beat, then it began to spin around. It transformed into the Grinch. A cheer went up from the guys in the living room, and another burst of energy roared down the stairs.

That one was Kellan.

"What's going on?" I asked him.

"It's me."

"What is?"

"The prophecy."

I frowned. *"What prophecy?"*

"The one that said you were going to be killed."

"The what *that says my sister is going to be killed?"* Damien roared.

I could feel Kellan's instant irritation, but I couldn't focus there because the first black mist had zipped outside the house. Kellan tore after him, blasting through the front door with enough force that the wood exploded.

"Fuck!"

"What was that?"

Damien came into the room, pushing his way through the crowd to my side. "What's going on?"

I opened my mouth to tell him what I knew, when we heard, "Uh…"

We turned.

Crowman was still there, still holding his beer, his eyes skirting from Damien to me. His shoulders lifted up and down on a deep sigh, and a look of resignation came over him. "You guys are doing your thing again, aren't you?"

Damien frowned, his eyebrows pulling together. "Um…"

Crowman shook his head, handing his beer to Damien. "Here, dude. You need this more than me. I'm out of here. Call me when it's safe for us humans."

Damien took the beer, and Crowman left, not rushing. There was a defeated look to him, his shoulders hunched as he moved through the stampede.

Damien turned back. "Did he just—"

Then Kellan yelled in our heads, *"SHAY!"*

Damien and I both jumped. We'd forgotten for a brief second.

"Kellan, where are you?" I asked.

"In the back."

We took off.

The house was still emptying, and people ran in every direction, including the backyard. A crowd had formed when we got there, and we pushed through.

At the front I could see two floating black veils of mist trading blows. Kellan was still non-corporeal.

"What are you doing?" I asked him.

"How do you kill it?" Damien added.

"I can't."

"What? Why not?" I demanded.

The thinner black mist swerved, and the larger black mist

countered. They weren't forming hands, just bunches of black mist as they hit each other.

"*What is that?*" Damien shrieked.

I could feel Kellan's reluctance, but I was losing patience. "*Kellan!*"

He sighed. "*It's me.*"

"What?" Damien squawked out loud before flushing, rolling his eyes, and asking in our heads, "*What?*"

"*My father lied to me. He got me to cross the boundary to the Underworld so a part of my darkness could separate from me.*"

My mouth dropped. "*Wha...*"

Damien said, "*Okay. What can we do now?*"

"*I have no idea.*" Kellan struck again.

The black mist dodged but then stopped and turned. I felt its attention, and it shrieked in all of our heads. "*YOU!*"

"*Oh, fuck.*" Damien mumbled.

The black mist lunged for me, zipping in a flash.

I stepped back as Kellan roared, "*NO!*"

From there, three things happened at once.

There was a giant *BOOM*.

Kellan lunged forward, toward himself.

And I threw up my hands, not knowing what to do.

Blinding light erupted from me.

I felt it leaving my body—soul, hands, arms, and every inch of me. I closed my eyes as it happened.

Then there was silence.

Sweet, blissful silence, and I cracked an eye open...not seeing anything at first. Blinding white light spread all around. I felt like I was inside a cloud.

"*Kellan?*"

Silence.

"*Damien?*"

Silence.

Oh no.

"Welcome."

I didn't know who said that, but I felt a strange sense of familiarity. Out of the white mist, a form came forward.

I frowned.

It was, well, a he-she. He was male, but he was also female, and they smiled at me.

"I am you, Shay."

"Me?"

They nodded, such kindness coming from them. *"We are you. We are your messenger spirit. You have extracted us to defend yourself against a part of your soulmate's darkness.*

"It'll be fine. We are stronger than your soulmate's darkness—at least this one that got loose from him. As we are speaking, he is binding his darkness back to himself. You are helping him. We are helping him, because he didn't know this could happen. We are instructing him.

I felt a pinch in my chest.

"That's the binding. It is coming into your soul bond. There's no other way."

"What's happening exactly?" I asked.

"Your mate has neglected his darkness for too long, but it's a part of him. He's tried to live among the humans as you do. It is hard on him. A portion of him suffers, and he's begun to unravel on the inside. His father felt it happening, took advantage, and helped move forward more unraveling. Your mate's darkness can do the father's bidding, and that bidding is to destroy you. With you gone, he'll get his son back, but he's not aware of the ramifications if that ever happens."

I swallowed hard. That didn't sound good. *"What are those ramifications?"*

"Total destruction of the universe."

Oh...okay then.

"Your bond is woven too deep. If you were to be extinguished, Kellan's pain would be too much. He wouldn't return to his father, as

is assumed. He would destroy everything. The pain would be intolerable, and yes, your soulmate is powerful enough to bring about the destruction of the universe. His power would be unmatched, except by a few."

"I didn't know Kellan was that powerful."

"He's a full demon, but he grows more powerful the longer he is bound to you. He has woven your bond so tightly that if you were ever killed, he would take all of your power. You both have pockets of strength that neither of you is aware of. He would seek those pockets and empty them. It would be enough to end the universe."

My head swam with all this information, and the figure broke off into two parts. One female. The other male. The male stepped forward, and both spoke out loud at the same time. "We are both you: the feminine and the masculine. We are your pure goodness and your celestial spirit. We are here to guide you, instruct you, and protect you. We are you, but we are your human guides as well. We are all-knowing. The binding is almost done. We will join with you again, but to prevent this from happening again, your soulmate must be allowed to be himself. To deny oneself is to starve oneself. The universe survives on both sides of the pendulum. Each side needs to fulfill its destiny."

"What does that mean...?" I trailed off.

There was another flash of light and a sudden burst of wind. It came at me all at once. I felt like a part of me had been stretched thin to stand apart, and now I was whole again.

I opened my eyes, finding myself once again in the backyard of Damien's fraternity house, but it wasn't Kellan staring at me. Or at least, it wasn't the Kellan I knew.

Panic lurched up in me, seizing my throat. "What just happened?"

CHAPTER 10

A DOUBLY EVIL KELLAN

I raced against time, chasing after myself, after Shay, and then time stopped.

He'd made a lunge for her, intent on shredding her from the inside out, when she threw up a hand, and everything paused.

I fell back, feeling the force of her power as it seeped into me—both of me—and a pure essence materialized. It was Shay's soul. I was held immobile. My other self was held paralyzed, and a needle appeared, much like the scythe that had appeared to me in the Underworld. Glowing light from Shay's essence began to weave the separated thread into me, her light helping to infuse it.

It burned into my soul as the needle moved in and out. In and out.

This wasn't entirely Shay, but it *was* her, joining the separation back to me with herself attached. The pain of her essence helped return that thread to me, not by its own spirit, but with her power infused.

It was painful, like surgery without anesthesia, but in the end, this extra power from her seeped into my being. I couldn't explain it, but I had so much power, I was engulfed in it. It was everywhere. In me. Behind me. In front of me. Above. Beneath.

It stretched as far as the world I could see, and I saw it all.

It was all within my grasp. I could reach out and take it—that easy.

But I knew that wasn't the truth. It was just a feeling, the false sensation of being the ruler over all kingdoms, my father's included. It was intoxicating and heady, but I knew there was a caveat. Every cell in my being wanted to seize it, take it, control it, and do what I wanted with it.

But I did nothing, and after a moment, time slowly restarted again.

I returned to where we'd been, and everything was the same.

Except it wasn't.

I was different. I was *more*.

I looked, and Shay was there. She was more too.

There was an otherworldly glow to her, and I felt it inside of me, too. I was the mirror to her. The opposite of whatever she was, but we were connected, and we needed each other. If we didn't have the other, there would be complete and utter destruction.

I didn't understand it, but I knew it.

I breathed it, and it was there.

I needed her to ground me as if I were a human who needed air.

I started for her, and she cocked her head to the side.

"You're different."

Her words echoed inside my heart chamber.

It was a jolt, but it felt like a purring sensation. A caress. I liked it.

I moved closer. "So are you."

I reached for her, feeling her inside, but needing to feel her on the outside.

There was a cough next to us.

Right.

We hadn't been alone when this happened, and we weren't alone now.

We blinked, almost as one. I could see out of Shay's eyes, and I knew she could see through mine.

Damien's eyebrows almost touched his hairline. A crowd of Damien's fraternity brothers and their friends from the party gaped at us. Except for two. One guy was funneling a beer. A girl was imagining me naked. Those two were fine.

Damien closed his eyes. *"How the hell is this going to be explained?"*

Suddenly Christmas music filled the air, coming from the second floor of the house, and everyone turned to look. Crowman appeared, a hose in hand, and he waved it from side to side. Fake snow rained down on everyone.

"Merry Christmas, bitches!" he yelled. "Welcome to the Alpha Mu house, where our live entertainment is out of this world. You ain't getting this from any other house. Now, everyone, get drunk and pretend we're all slutty Christmas angels together."

There was a pause.

Then a smattering of laughs.

A girl sighed. "Oh, thank God it was all a show. I thought I was on a *seriously* bad trip for a minute."

"You and me both, girl."

More awkward and relieved laughing sprinkled through the crowd, and slowly, one by one, they moved back inside, leaving just Damien, Shay, and myself in the yard.

Crowman turned off the fake snow and propped the hose on his shoulder. He lifted a foot to rest on the deck railing in front of him. He shook his head, staring down at us. "I'd like to request that you two don't attend our next holiday party. I can only handle learning that humans aren't alone in this world so many times. I keep hoping I'll forget, but you're making that shit hard."

He disappeared inside.

"What the fuck happened?" Damien asked. "You both look seriously weird. It's like you're glowing with neon light, like a backdrop behind yourself. It's freaking me out, and I'm not human. That shouldn't freak me out." He held his hands up, backing toward the house. "Do me a favor. This time, I don't want to know. I want to pretend I'm only a fraternity brother tonight."

With that, he turned around and went inside.

The music went up a few notches.

Shay almost floated to me.

I looked down, but her feet were there.

She seemed less human than she had before. And I certainly didn't know what I was anymore.

She gave me a serene and loving smile, placing a hand on my cheek. "It's a Christmas miracle."

"That it is." I chuckled.

We both knew that wasn't the truth.

But at this moment, I was just relieved the prophecy hadn't been a prophecy.

"I love you."

"I love you, too," she said, drawing me close. "Let's figure it out tomorrow."

I groaned. "I'm down for that."

CHAPTER 11

CHRISTMAS IS STILL NOT KELLAN'S FAVORITE

These humans. Such simpletons.

They brought trees into their living rooms and put up lights. They sang the same songs every year, most of them sacrilegious—about altars and sacrifices made.

Demons *are* the better species. We're simple. We give in and enjoy and relish in our pleasures—

"Kellan?"

"Yes, dear?" I turned, my drink in hand.

A slight smile turned up the corners of Shay's mouth when she saw my drink. "I see you're enjoying the festivities."

"What?" I looked down.

It was a red drink, garnished with some mint leaves and a red and white candy cane hanging off the end. I shifted, my chest slightly tight. I blamed my soulmate's pure joy in attending these parties for that. She'd insisted we follow the dress code, so I was in all cream. I'm a *demon.* Dark grey was my favorite.

Shay pressed into me, her hand touching my chest and her arm circling behind. Her eyes grew soft, and she tilted her head back. That smile softened as well, matching the glow on her face. The glow that I put there. You know...on account of my amazing skills in bed.

Yes. I was confident in my prowess in bed.

All conceited thoughts aside, I took a moment to enjoy the feeling of Shay against me.

She loved these humans, this world.

It wasn't my first choice. *She* was my first choice. Always would be, no matter who appeared against us, what battle was on the forefront. It was always Shay.

We were at one of her college friends' parties. We had another to attend after this, one of her professors. And tomorrow we'd travel with Damien to see their family for the holiday break.

Since what happened the other night, Shay and I had a talk. I was to indulge periodically in my deeper bases of death and destruction—but no humans. That was Shay's stipulation.

So, on my holiday break, I'd be killing demons.

I was salivating already, thinking about it.

It would kill two birds with one stone—satisfying my demon instincts and also making me an even bigger pain in my father's ass. He'd messed with me. He'd tried to take Shay from me. In my eyes, the war was on.

My first move: to kill as many of his henchmen as I could.

It was my Christmas gift to myself, and Shay was on board.

But for now, we were here, and my job was to make her happy.

I ran a finger under her chin, tipping her head back to meet my gaze. As her eyes caught and held mine, and as I felt the punch I always did when we connected, I smiled down at her. "Happy?"

She melted into me, her eyes sparkling. "Amazingly so."

"Good." I dropped my head down, my mouth finding hers, and I counted the minutes until I could whisk her away. In the meantime, I'd satisfy myself by enjoying her mouth, no matter where we were.

I was a demon. I didn't give a fuck.

STILL KELLAN

Between you and me, I'm looking forward to the next holiday adventure.

I'm figuring it'll be Easter.

I hope you enjoyed Kellan and Shay's adventures.
Read <u>Evil</u> to learn their initial love story.

ALSO BY TIJAN

Paranormal Standalones and Series:

Evil

Micaela's Big Bad

The Tracker

Davy Harwood Series (paranormal)

Latest books:

A Dirty Business (Mafia, Kings of New York Series)

A Cruel Arrangement (Mafia, Kings of New York Series)

Aveke (Fallen Crest novella, standalone)

Fallen Crest and Crew Universe

Fallen Crest/Roussou Universe

Fallen Crest Series

Crew Series

The Boy I Grew Up With (standalone)

Rich Prick (standalone)

Frisco

Other series:

Broken and Screwed Series (YA/NA)

Jaded Series (YA/NA suspense)

Davy Harwood Series (paranormal)

Carter Reed Series (mafia)

The Insiders

Mafia Standalones:

Cole

Bennett Mafia

Jonah Bennett

Canary

Sports Romance Standalones:

Enemies

Teardrop Shot

Hate To Love You

The Not-Outcast

Hostile

Young Adult Standalones:

Ryan's Bed

A Whole New Crowd

Brady Remington Landed Me in Jail

College Standalones:

Antistepbrother

Kian

Contemporary Romances:

Bad Boy Brody

Home Tears

Fighter

Rockstar Romance Standalone:

Sustain

More books to come!

MICAELA'S BIG BAD

JAY HAPPENED

The only thing standing between me and me getting drunk was a naked four-year-old.

He was my best friend's nephew, and he was swinging his little penis in the air, staring at it, smiling and giggling, and clapping his hands with glee. He was also standing just inside the door, and I was standing on the doorstep, a full bottle of whiskey needing to be drank, and he wouldn't let me in.

"Heya, Bud."

More laughing.

He clapped.

He was shaking his little hips as if it were the first time he'd learned how to shake those hips.

"Bud."

That was actually his name.

"What?"

I nodded to the doorhandle. "Let me in."

"No." He hit the lock—shit, my hands were full, but why hadn't I just grabbed for the handle, anyway?—and took off running.

Crap.

I had a bulging backpack on me. Three grocery bags were hanging from one of my arms, the same one I had my coffee in. My other free hand held the whiskey. I knew my priorities. Also, the grocery bags were filled with my clothes, or at least what I had been able to grab in a desperate speed-round of packing.

I went so fast. If there was a speed packing race, I could've been a contender.

Not a winner, a contender. After all, I was realistic about my abilities.

The most extraordinary thing about me was my long hair. I had long dark hair.

Jay used to whisper how he liked to twine it in his hands when he—nope. Not going there.

But this was me. Micaela Nadeem, an energist who didn't use my energist side. Middle of the road. Some might say boring. I played everything safe. No risks in life. Not great at anything, but not bad at anything either.

Even leaving my boyfriend, I half-assed it. I took what I could, and bolted.

And I threw a fork.

I should've thrown a knife. At least a knife? Why not go totally lame and toss a spoon instead? Nope. A fork. I was a fork girl. A fork non-energist energist.

My car was full of blankets, what bathroom toiletries I'd been able to grab, and all my schoolwork, because this fork girl still needed to finish two courses before I had a bachelor's in communications. What I planned to do with that? I hadn't a clue. See my theme here.

I barely knew what I was going to do past tomorrow, so the future was totally up in the air.

I was not, what someone would call, a *planner*.

Who are those people?

They're a species I'll never understand.

I tried hitting the doorbell with my elbow.

Nothing. I chafed against the wall instead.

I tried a second time.

Rin—

It cut out.

Great.

I had two options. Put my stuff down, find my phone (I had no idea which bag I'd stuffed it in) and try her that way. Bud was here, so chances were high that Nikki was babysitting, but her phone always seemed off so the probability of that working was nil.

My other choice: "Nikki! *Nikki!* NIKKI!"

She came out from the back hallway, her shirt hanging down one arm, doing up her pants, and her hair was all frayed everywhere.

I—

I couldn't.

Not at all.

Her eyes went wide seeing me, and she cringed.

Her face was all red and splotchy.

Her lips swollen.

She came over, cursing under her breath, and unlocked the door. She opened the door, stepping back. I stepped in, and hissed under my own breath, "You just got laid! While you're babysitting!"

More cringing from her, but she shut both doors and swung around to me. "I—" She took in my bags, and surmised the contents in my bag, and her eyes got round all over again. "Oh no, Cale."

I wrinkled my nose at her. "Don't 'Cale' me in that tone. Babysitting. You! Bud locked the door on me."

"Bud?!" She whirled around.

And Bud decided to come running back down the hall, yelling at the top of his lungs, arms in the air. Still naked.

"Bud!" she gasped, rushing to him. "What are you doing here?"

She lunged right.

He jumped left.

She jumped left.

He dodged, then climbed up on a chair.

"BUD!"

Still giggling, he got up on the kitchen counter, and ran the length of it. He was fast approaching the point where he'd be caught or have to jump because across from him was the refrigerator.

I heard Nikki draw in a swift breath of air, at the exact same time as I held mine.

He launched—

"BU—"

He was caught mid-air by two muscular arms.

He was curled up to a very manly and shirtless chest, and he was carried the rest of the way into the living area where I was still standing, still holding all my bags, still clutching that whiskey because I was still hoping to crack this sucker open tonight and drown every last sorrow.

"Uncle Cream!" We were *still* on the high-pitched theme here. That was coming from Bud, and he was pulling with all his might at his Uncle Brad's hair.

There was a story behind why Brad was nicknamed Cream, but I never heard it—actually, I never wanted to hear it. I was hoping to go through my entire life not knowing...and now onto the weird family awkwardness here.

Brad and Nikki were not boyfriend/girlfriend, or at least I hadn't been updated on an official relationship status.

What they were, though, were siblings to Bud's parents. Nikki's sister married Brad's brother, and their first shindig that resulted in my best friend having to do up her pants happened the night their siblings were married.

Do the math.

Bud was four.

Nikki's sister didn't get preggo until the honeymoon.

Brad ending up in Nikki's bed, on and off, had been going on for a long-ass time. I say it like that because there are always after-shocks whenever Brad comes around.

Then, he would leave.

Nikki had tried closing up the bedsheets to him, but he could charm and seduce her and say all the nice words to her to get those sheets back opened pretty much any time he deemed her worthy.

He'd hotfoot out, and Nikki would get a text from one of our other girls (we had a lot around town), and there'd be a picture of Brad curled around another girl.

They were back and forth so much, and it'd been going on for almost four years.

This wasn't my drama, but I was her best friend, and I was pulling the best friend card and admitting only to myself that I was tired of the Brad-drama. Also, not shocked that he'd bring Bud around when he was hooking up with Nikki. How he got Bud into the house without Nikki seeing him before the bed-capades was something I also didn't want to know all the details about because Nikki was all looking shocked at seeing her nephew naked.

And in her house.

"What's up, Nadeem?"

I grimaced. "Don't speak to me."

Uncle Cream was the most real-life version of someone who reminded me of Billy Hargrove from *Stranger Things*. The difference was that Uncle Cream had straight hair, not curly hair. That was it. He could've been his twin, both physically and personality wise.

"Brad," Nikki snapped, but my best friend wasn't paying

much attention to her recent lay. She was back to looking at me. Studying my bags. Studying the booze in my hand.

She noticed before, but got distracted. She was back to noticing and she was figuring it out.

My best friend was catching up here.

"Jay?" she asked.

Nope. That most definitely wasn't a frog in my throat. And it hadn't doubled in size when I nodded back.

"Yeah," I rasped.

Another cringe from her, mixed with a pitying look. I hated the pitying look.

The frog just did a loud-ass *ribbit*.

I looked away, and shuffled back because I knew what was going to happen. She would herd Uncle Cream and Bud, no— she'd make sure Bud got clothes on first—and once they were gone, she'd take my whiskey from me. She'd go to the kitchen. She'd pull out some drink glasses, put in some of the nice cubed ice she always keeps on hand for me, and we'd pour ourselves a drink. After that, it'd either be a veg-out night, which I was now wondering how that phrase came about? Because we'd sit, talk, fill each other in, and we'd drink. Pizza would either get ordered, or we'd go the other way.

We'd drink. Talk. And decide we needed to go out.

It was Halloween, a night we both avoided because we were usually insulted by how humans viewed us, but... Jay happened.

Read the rest of Micaela's Big Bad!

DAVY HARWOOD

1

"Mr. Moser is not happy."

That was my greeting as I dropped my books on the library table and plopped down next to my roommate. She was the originator of my stupid hotline volunteer career. The career that was *finito*, done, and over with. I snuck inside that morning, slipped the envelope underneath the door, and bolted.

There are occasions where I'm very much a coward, and this was one of those times.

"I'm not surprised," I muttered and bent to grab a pencil out of my bag. The location of the bag was just opportune. It was on the floor so I was able to turn and present my back to my roommate. I hoped she'd take the hint.

"What do you mean you're not surprised? Why aren't you surprised?" Emily hadn't taken the hint. Then again, she never did.

She had been my roommate for the last three months. Her entire life plan was written in detail with bulleted expenditure costs, but it all revolved around her career choice in social work. She was the one to volunteer at the hotline. She was the one who dragged me there. She was even the one that pointed out Adam. Emily wasn't the reason why I stayed. Adam was that reason.

I like boys. Most people would say that I'm boy-crazy, but the truth is I just find them entertaining. I would never ever kill myself over a guy. They're not worth that much, but they are worth a fun activity or a cuddle during a movie. When I saw his rich chestnut hair and almond eyes, I knew that Adam would make a great movie-cuddler.

"Davina!" Emily called out sharply. She was being ignored. That made her pissy.

I sighed and fought the urge to bury my head in my book. No. Why fight it? I buried my head into my book and groaned dramatically. I knew one thing. It would make Emily shut up. If there was one thing that made her uncomfortable, it was when someone was in need of emotional reassurance. I once saw her spill a drink and use that as an excuse to leave a group when one of the girls started crying. I highly doubted Emily's social work career would make it past the paper it was written on, but I wasn't going to be the one to tell her.

On another note, I hated being called Davina. It's Davy. It'll always be Davy. It'll never be Davina. Then I realized there was silence. Emily had quieted. I risked a look, and saw that her eyes were downcast on her own pile of books. I thanked my own quick wits for this reprieve.

"Davina."

I stiffened at the name, but when I looked over my shoulder I melted into a gooey feeling inside. Adam was approaching with an eager stride. His almond eyes sharpened with warmth, and I saw the earnest grin on his face. Tall, dark, and just pretty. That's how I'd describe my perfect guy, and Adam easily fit the bill. Plus, he wore Abercrombie. What girl didn't like that? Well, probably a lot, but it looked yummy on him.

"Hi, Adam." I was warm. I was always warm around him.

He stood at the end of our table and seemed riveted by me. I wondered why and then let it go. Obviously, the guy had woken up and realized his love for me.

"I heard about the suicide last night. Are you okay? You were there, right? That's what Shelly said."

Shelly. All the gooeyness dried up. Shelly was my competition. I cheated on my empath rules and took a peek inside her once. The feeling was mutual. She hated me even more and I didn't need to be psychic to know that she planned to murder me.

I was only joking...somewhat.

I was a short girl at five foot six inches with an average build, not slim, but not big either. I had brown curls on a good day, and a frizzy fray on a bad, but I knew my dark brown eyes and my full lips were my best features. Guys liked to stare at both of them, but Shelly was a tall willowy blonde with absolutely beautiful blue eyes. I always felt like I was swimming in a lake when I looked at them.

Shelly liked Adam. I liked Adam, but I wasn't sure who Adam liked.

"What else did Shelly say?" I couldn't hide my sarcasm.

Adam's smile dimmed slightly, but he pressed, "Is it true? You answered the phone and she was on the roof?"

The boy was goal oriented. "Yes. I was there, but she jumped."

Emily looked up with wide eyes. Adam shifted a little and his eyes skirted from me to Emily. "Are you... are you okay? Shelly said that you quit the hotline."

Emily harrumphed.

"Um..."

"I can't believe you quit." Emily had to put her two cents in.

"Yeah, I mean..." Adam took the seat next to mine and lowered his voice. It was soothing and seductive to my ears. "I mean...the place won't be the same without you, you know?"

Of course I knew, but that was the point of it. I wanted to get as far away as possible. It would always remind me of the girl from last night. I wasn't freaked out with agony and so forth, but the truth was that I was freaked out by the gut-wrenching feeling that something worldly awful had happened and that it was connected to me. "I just... it's too much, you know? I can't handle—she died in front of me. I can't...it's just too much for me."

I saw the sympathy in Adam. He placed his hand on mine. "I know exactly what you mean. If you ever need anything, call me. Okay? I want to help you through this tough time."

Emily fled the scene. I almost caught a back draft from her sprint. "I'd really like that, Adam."

He squeezed my hand. "Any time. Remember that, Davina."

I'd remind him another time not to call me that name.

Then the happily-ever-after feeling was gone as I felt a vampire walk past us. A cold wind slapped my insides and I looked up. Normally, vamps ignore me. They can't feel me like I can feel them so they just believe that they're not noticed.

Not this time.

I gasped when I saw a pair of coal-black eyes staring right back at me. The vamp was tall with jet black hair. He wore a white buttoned-down shirt over jeans. He kept going, but I still felt his eyes after he turned the corner.

"Davina," Adam said sharply, confused.

"What...what were you saying?" His hand was gone. I wanted his hand back.

"I..." He frowned again and asked, "Are you okay? You pushed me away and I mean, that's okay if that's what you need right now. I just thought..." He trailed off and looked away.

I didn't have to be empathic to see his insecurity. "It's not that. That guy scared me just now. I'm sorry. I want your help, I really do."

His eyes twinkled.

I sighed again. How could any girl not fall in love with how adorable he was?

"Can you two stop with the sappy moment?" Emily returned with a storm at her backside. She slumped in her seat. "I'm trying to study."

"Oh, yeah," Adam laughed, a little embarrassed. "I-uh—I'll talk to you later, Davina?"

I nodded. Hell yeah, we'd talk.

"Good. See you later then."

I glanced at Emily as he left and saw her sharp green eyes on me. She narrowed them in disgust.

"You make me sick."

"What? Why?" I was innocent.

"You totally lied to him just now. I had to run to the bathroom to keep from barfing. Really?! You can't handle it? She died in front of you? Mr. Moser told me that you need to get back to the hotline. You broke protocol and that's why you quit, not because you're 'emotionally shaken.' Seriously, Davina."

Maybe my roommate knew me a little better than I realized.

"Can you blame me?! Adam is to die for." I could not believe I just said those words.

"I can't believe you said that." Emily reiterated my thoughts.

I flushed, embarrassed, and leaned back in my chair. "What am I supposed to do? I didn't quit because of protocol, okay? And I need any advantage with Adam. You know Shelly Whistworth has her claws in him."

Emily was annoyed. "You have to go and talk to Mr. Moser. You did break the rules and he's worried about a lawsuit. And Adam Darley is not worth your time to lie and lower yourself. If he's a stand-up guy, he'll recognize that you're much more fun to be with than Shelly Witless. If he's not and he goes to her, he's not the guy that you'll want anyway."

"I'm not lowering myself," I remarked, and crossed my arms. "I'm just being manipulative."

Emily looked at me knowingly. "Well, stop. It's annoying."

"It's fun."

Emily opened her mouth and started to say something, but I felt the blast of cold race through me. My heart slowed as the vamp walked towards me from the opposite direction. His eyes were on me again. He seemed to look right through me, but he didn't slow his pace. He walked right past.

I hated vampires. I knew what they could do from personal experience. However, there were a lot of good vampires that liked to hang out on campus. Some of them even took classes and wanted to learn. This guy looked like a regular college student and he walked like one. Right to the computer lab, and back out again for a Mountain Dew. Typical college behavior, but I was betting he wasn't one of the 'good' vampires.

"Do you know who that is?"

"You interrupted me. I was talking."

I watched as he returned from the vending machines and sat back down at a computer. "That guy. Do you know him?"

"We're at a school with six thousand students. Really?! We're freshmen, Davina. How can you expect that I'd know him?"

I turned and regarded her. "Do you know him or not?"

She shifted uncomfortably in her seat.

"Who is he, Emily?" I leaned closer and hoped he couldn't hear us. There were two glass walls between us and the computer lab always buzzed with conversations and printing papers. If he tuned in, he could hear us, but for once I hoped that I wasn't a speck on this guy's radar. Correction—make that this vampire's radar.

"He's in my social work class."

"Intro?"

"Yeah. He's a junior and he's fulfilling a requirement." She sounded like she'd practiced that. Something felt off with her.

She liked to share her opinions on people, but she didn't with this guy.

"You like him." I couldn't fault her. Vamps had seductive appeal down to perfection. Emily was a girl. Even *she* would fall under their power whether they intended it or not. The only way you could fight against their pull is if you knew what they were.

"I do not!" Emily cried out. She started to gather her books back up, but I laid a hand on them.

"It's okay. He's dreamy. I understand." I glanced back over, but sighed in disgust.

He just sat there at the computer. His hands didn't move on the keyboard. "Who is he?" I asked again, still watching the back of his head.

He sat rigidly.

"Luke Roane," Emily sighed. She'd be mortified at how dreamy it sounded.

"Roane?" I arched my eyebrows.

What kind of name was that? I'd heard of a Roane back home, but the name was only spoken about as a legend. Most of the vamps didn't believe he existed. I didn't like this new twist. My college life wasn't supposed to deal with supernatural things like this. I wanted an Adam in my life, not a vampire named Roane.

"He's really intelligent." Emily had opened her floodgates. Now her opinions flew freely. "He cares about the world and he's got some super insights into humanity."

I bet he did.

"Even Professor Sulls asks his opinions on matters. Luke's like no other guy that I know. I mean, I respect him. I have really high standards and I only respect two other guys," she said, casually.

"I know." I said dryly, "Jesus and Martin Luther King Jr."

"Can you believe it?" Emily sighed again. She was on the

fast track for her first college lovecrush. It was my little name for those crushes when a girl thinks she's in love. They were annoying... to everybody.

Lovecrushes aside—or maybe front and center—I hadn't moved my eyes off Roane's back, but then my eyes slid past his shoulders to his black computer screen. I found myself staring smack head-on with him. I gasped in mortification. He'd been staring right at me the whole time. This was not good, not at all. He knew that I knew. I knew that he knew I knew. I could've pretended that I didn't know he was listening to us, but now all bets were off.

He'd seen.

I smiled smugly and whispered, "I know what you are."

His face didn't move. His eyes didn't react, but I knew I'd made him angry.

––––––––––––

Read the rest of Davy Harwood!